MONTANA, HERE I BE!

by

Dan Cushman

The Golden West Large Print Books
Long Preston, North Yorkshire,
BD23 4ND, England.

British Library Cataloguing in Publication Data.

Cushman, Dan
    Montana, here I be!

    A catalogue record of this book is
    available from the British Library

    ISBN   978-1-84262-913-0 pbk

First published 1950

Published in Large Print 2012 by arrangement with
Golden West Literary Agency.

The Golden West Large Print is an imprint of Library Magna
Books Ltd.

Printed and bound in Great Britain by
T.J. (International) Ltd., Cornwall, PL28 8RW

CONTENTS

Chapter One

Hangin' An Imposter

Mountain darkness was a long time in coming, but the black-whiskered man showed no impatience. He remained in the saddle, his body slouched to one side, his jaw slowly revolving around a chaw of tobacco while he looked at the gold camp of American Flag spread across the flats of the Missouri River beneath him.

He was about forty, shorter and broader than most men. He had long arms and easy-hanging shoulders; his skin was burned coffee-brown from many years of Western sun. He wore a black slouch hat, sweat-stained and crusted with dust; his shirt was Cree buckskin with most of the beadwork gone; his homespun trousers were thrust in the tops of scuffed jackboots. Around his waist hung a brace of Navy Colts on crossed belts.

He sat with perfect patience while sunset faded and shadows spread from the mountain draws across the river flats. Lights began to show – in saloons and dance halls along the camp's main street, in cabins beside the sluices that operated night and day. Something that looked like a torchlight parade moved along one of the streets. His eyes narrowed a trifle and he chawed more slowly. It looked like some sort of celebration. News of a victory, maybe for General McClellan. He spat at the thought. Nothing but a Northern victory would get a celebration out of American Flag – it was that sort of a camp.

At last the twilight grew thick enough to suit him, so he nudged his gunpowder-roan pony and picked a zigzag path through rocks and windfalls down the mountainside. It was almost dark when he emerged from jack timber and rode through the planless assortment of cabins, wickiups, and Conestoga wagons that formed the residential district. A flume passed over the road, dripping water on him as he rode below. His first glimpse of the main street confirmed his impression that this was no ordinary night in American Flag. A steady press of bull drivers and miners jammed the street.

He saw a freckled kid toting a bucket of water, and nudged the pony over beside him. 'Seems like a brisk evenin' in this gold camp, son,' he said in a voice as careless as his appearance. 'What's all the excitement? Be there a new gold strike, or have them sneakin' Yankees gone and took Richmond?'

The Civil War was too distant to interest the boy. 'Plenty more'n the capture of any town of Richmond, mister. Guess we're about to see the biggest thing that's took place in Montana Territory since she seceded from Idaho. There's goin' to be a hangin'.'

'A hangin'?' The black-whiskered man jerked his head in a sign of disappointment. He aimed tobacco juice at a piece of quartz and plastered it dead center. 'What kind o' small-bore village ye got here, anyhow? All this excitement with torches and flambeaux on account o' one measly hangin'. Why down in Californy whar I come from you couldn't get the boys to stir from their faro game for less'n a double.'

'American Flag ain't takin' a back seat to Californy, mister. Fact is, this camp's doing something tonight that Californy wanted to do for ten years and couldn't. You see, this here ain't any ordinary hangin'.'

'No-o?'

'No, sir, it ain't.' He was proud of American Flag, a camp that the editor of *The Sluice Box* had been referring to as 'the golden diadem of the Rockies', and he took the opportunity to swagger a little. 'You can just bet it ain't any ordinary hangin'. Tonight the vigilance committee is hangin' *Comanche John*.'

'Waal, now!' The whiskered man received the news and spent some time chawing it over. His eyes were narrowed as he regarded the boy. He was serious, all right. He meant what he said. Tonight they were hanging Comanche John. 'You mean Comanche John

9

the famous road agent that steals from the rich and gives to the pore – that brave, hard-ridin' Californy holdup man they made up that song about?'

'Naw, sir, I mean the trigger-pullin', killin', bushwhackin' wolf-varmint that robbed the Last Chance coach last night and kilt two of the passengers off'n her without giving 'em any more chance than a decent man would give a couple of stray cats.'

Obviously he was quoting from his elders, so this was a fair sample of the sentiment in American Flag.

The whiskered man said, 'It's an outrage, killing men without giving 'em a chance! I must say, though, that it don't sound like the Comanche John I heered about. More like something that'd be pulled by that sinful vigilance committee down at Virginny City.'

'You don't need to claim we ain't hangin' the real Comanche John! Where you from, Last Chance? They're always trying to belittle us here in American Flag.'

'I'm from a heap further'n Last Chance.'

That mollified him a little. 'Well, anyhow, we're hangin' him.'

'By grab, don't know what's coming over the world. Never expected to hear that the old Comanche would shoot men without giving 'em a chance. But if he done it, he done it, and I say he deserved to git hung. What's more, I say he deserves to git hung

10

with a rough rope.'

'Don't you worry about *this* camp hangin' him right.'

'Just tell me this – did the old curly wolf put up much of a battle before they took him?'

'Naw! He was yalla and came in meek as a lamb. They all come meek when Cap'n Brass goes after 'em.'

'Cap'n Brass,' the whiskered man repeated. The name might have meant something to him. He scratched through his whiskers and looked far off. 'So the Cap'n is a rough one?'

'Rough as cactus with her hide on.'

'Head of the vigilance committee, you say?'

'Yep. You'll find nothin' second-rate or ornery in *this* camp.'

'Whar's Brass got the culprit chained up?'

'In the skookum house.'

He pointed out the jail, or the flat roof of it, just visible over lower buildings. The whiskered man thanked him and nudged his pony into movement, a wary wolf trot, picking a winding course among freight wagons and long strings of mules, and then through the crowd that overflowed the walks into the town's rutty streets. The brim of his black slouch hat shaded his face, and his eyes kept shifting, his hands never far from the butts of his Navy Colts.

No one paid the least attention to him, and finally he reined in with a newly built gallows blocking his way.

11

It was a fine job. Lots of camps were satisfied with such makeshifts as the ridgepole of an unfinished house or the wide-spreading limb of a cottonwood, but American Flag was first class. This gallows was made of sawed plank, it had a high platform and a trap, the pole with its crossmember was twenty feet high, and its permanence showed that the builders expected it to be used again and again.

The whiskered man swung down and led his horse across a walk and down a passage between a saloon and a Chinese washee. The irregular alleyway beyond was heaped with bottles and other refuse, but there was nothing to block a quick departure if he needed to make one. He scrutinized it at some length, fixing the picture in his mind, then he fastened the bridle reins to some log butts at the rear of the saloon and slouched back to the main street.

There he fell in beside a weather-burned prospector and said, 'Got to hand it to the old Comanche, he sure packs 'em in. I don't reckon there'd be a bigger crowd turn out iffen they was to hang the Honorable Jefferson Davis, President of the Confederate States of America.'

'Too bad we can't hang 'em both. Jeff Davis and Comanche John – two polecats doing a rope dance on the same limb – now there's my idea of a satisfyin' night's entertainment.'

12

The whiskered man grunted something and moved on without continuing the conversation. The sidewalks were made of pine poles laid corduroy fashion without trimming, and their round tops made walking a little difficult, especially for a man who's been spavined by long hours in the saddle.

'Jeff Davis and Comanche John on the same limb. And already they've kilt off old Stonewall Jackson. By grab, what's the world comin' to?'

He walked from saloon to saloon, working his way through crowds of men, and paused beneath the pole awning of a large two-story structure bearing a windflapped banner that read: *The White Palace*. A blind man was seated on an upended hogshead, aimlessly thrumming the strings of a banjo. After a time spent gazing with white, sightless eyes over the heads of the crowd he commenced singing in a husky but musically appealing voice:

'Co-man-che John is a highwayman,
He came from County Pike
With a pal called Henry Singleshot
And one named Injun Ike;
They drifted out to Kansas
In the year of fifty-three
To fight in the election
On the side of slaver-ee.

'John then lit out for Yuba town
With a pal named Jimmy Dale,
And just for some excitement
They robbed the Eastern mail.
Now Jimmy's six foot underground
And much he rues the day
And Comanche rides the long cou-lee
Tryin' to git away.'

The blind man commanded silence as long as he sang, but with the last twang of the banjo a drunken miner yipped, 'You'll be writin' another verse for that song after tonight, White-Eyes. The Comanche will have the longest neck of any dirty road agent in the Territory about half an hour from now, I'm thinkin'.'

The blind man's voice rolled out, addressing the empty night over the speaker's head.

'The wrong man's neck, that's what'll be taking the kinks out of vigilante rope tonight. Nobody can tell me that Comanche John would blast down two men just for the fun of hearing his Navies go *bang*. And you can't tell me that Cap'n Brass and his yalla-dog pack o' vigilante stranglers would be the men to take him. No, sir, not ten to one they wouldn't.'

'I hear tell he shoots two guns with his hands and one with his foot, how about that, White-Eyes?'

Other miners were jeering at White-Eyes

now, and more kept crowding around to enjoy the sport.

'Why don't you run Comanche John for President?' somebody called out. Then he added, 'Run him for President o' the Confederacy.'

'White-Eyes, sing us that song about the time down in Californy when he filled up your banjo with gold and gave it to you for Christmas.'

'Yes, sometime I'll write a song about that, but right now if you want I'll tell it to ye!' The blind man stood atop the hogshead. He was tall, and it brought his head in contact with the pole awning. There was an ominous quality about him, his head bent forward, his eyes shining milky and sightless in the half-light. One glance at him made the noisiest drunk in the crowd quiet down and listen in spite of himself. White-Eyes waited with a fine dramatic instinct, and at the right moment he began to speak.

'It was like this. There I was, ridin' on the Nevada City coach. It was about dark, they said, them as could see, and the road was on the switchbacks right where she crosses the pass at Three Pines. There was a shotgun guard up beside the driver, but he didn't make more fuss than a pink bunny at a rattlesnake's reunion when this black-whiskered gent showed himself in the middle of the road.

'I couldn't see him, a-course, but I could hear his voice, and live to the end o' time I'll never forget it. "Toss down the strong box," he says. "I'm Comanche John and I swore off killin' shotgun guards all week. The week's five days gone," he says, "and I don't want to break my resolution, so keep your hands innocent and thank your mother's prayers that ye caught me in a pious mood, because I'm a ring-tailed roarer from the Rawhide Mountains and I get jittery as a snake rattle when I ain't had my man for breakfast."

'Yes, sir, as I stand here on this bar'l, them was the old Comanche's words. All alone he was, and not a swaybacked son of all them on the coach so much as lifted a derringer. Took 'em clean right down to their last wallet. When he got to me, John says, "You be blind, ain't ye?" And I says, "Blind I be, ever since the Sacramento fire of fifty-one." Well, gents, the old Comanche took my banjo and rode off with it together with the rest of the swag, but four days later, right on my bed in Lucky Maud's hotel down at Nevada City, I found that banjo.' He lifted the instrument for them to see. 'This same banjo I hold hyar tonight. But it wasn't the same as when he took it. Heavy it was, gents – so heavy I couldn't lift it. Filled with nuggets of gold. Yaller nuggets the size of Yankee lies. You hear that, you dirty abolitionists? He'd filled her with gold and gave it back to me. That's the sort of a gent

Comanche John is.'

The drunken miner shouted, 'Well I notice they got the Comanche belly-crawlin' tonight.'

'Ain't enough vigilante stranglers betwixt here and the bedrock of hell to make Comanche John belly-crawl. It ain't him they're stranglin'. It's some pore pilgrim that got in the way of Cap'n Brass's freight outfit, from the talk I hear.'

The black-whiskered man could no longer restrain himself. 'Glory be, that's what I been suspectin' all along. Them Yankee vigilantes are hangin' an imposter.'

White-Eyes had started to say something and checked himself. Other men were shouting. He waved his arms trying to silence them. 'Who was it said that? Wait a minute, gents. Quiet downt I heered him, I tell you. I heered him right then. Comanche John.' Half a dozen men were heehawing and he shouted above them. 'When I hear a voice I never forget it. I tell ye, that was Comanche John.'

Scarcely a person there knew which of the many voices he'd had reference to, and they wouldn't have believed him, anyway. The black-whiskered man slouched up, drew a hand from his pocket, and opened it over the banjo, letting a nugget fall. It was big as the end of his thumb, and torchlight falling on it made a reflection the deep color of gold from Bannack.

'Sure, White-Eyes,' he muttered from the side of his mouth. 'Sure it was Comanche John, and we'll have a little something to say to that stranglin' committee before they get to pullin' the kinks from their rope, won't we?'

White-Eyes stared beyond him, grinning. He didn't say a word. He thrust the nugget deep in his old gray jeans and commenced whanging the banjo, stamping his boots atop the hogshead, singing in a wild voice:

'Co-man-che rode from Yuba town
In the merry month of May
To rob the bank at Oroville
And a stagecoach on the way;
The yaller gold came easy
And he spent it twice as free
He'd always stake a pore blind man
Wherever he might be.'

Others tossed coins and small nuggets of gold to White-Eyes, then the crowd broke up, and the whiskered man moved with the main stream, careless, his thumbs hooked in the band of his homespuns just above his pistol-heavy scabbards.

'Cap'n Brass,' he muttered. 'The stranglin' Cap'n Brass. That'd be him as sure as judgment.'

He walked past the gallows and spat at it. He'd never had a fancy for the things. There was less excitement at the lower end of the street. He could see the river's surface, shining like metal, the current gurgling swift and cold through the rowboat docks. No steamboats there, eighty miles above the Great Falls. American Flag was reached by freight road from Fort Benton, head of river navigation, or by the long route up from Salt Lake.

One of the buildings was fitted with an improvised steeple, and a banner was strung across the front. He squinted at it from several angles and stopped a miner to say, 'Would ye mind readin' that sign for a pore pilgrim whose education never went so far as to include the three R's?'

'It says, "Repent Ye Sinners or Ye'll Roast in Hell"'

The whiskered man heehawed and slapped dust from the legs of his pants. 'That's him, I'll lay gold coin agin' worthless greenbacks it is. That's the Parson! What's he look like? Is he a long, lean old buzzard with a windpipe like a plucked rooster's?'

The man said he looked like that, that he called himself Reverend Jeremiah Parker, and at present he was probably giving solace to the condemned man, Comanche John. 'They were friends, the Parson and John, so I hear,' he said. 'Seems like a funny combine to me – a road agent and a preacher.'

'Now, hold on. I hear this Comanche John ain't so bad. From the word I got, he generally shoots varmints in need of such and lifts gold off coaches so heavy-loaded it's cruel to the horses. O'course I never met this famous road agent face to face, but when I was over in Orofino I heered a mule skinner singing a song that said–'

'Comanche John is a back-shootin', green-bellied rattlesnake and he deserves to git hung. Fact, he's *going* to git hung, and by the looks of things yonder up the street he's going to git hung right now.'

A man was on the gallows, lighting a pitch basket, drawing it aloft on a length of chain. Others saw it and came from everywhere. When the black-whiskered man got there, a shoving, boot-stamping crowd was close around the platform. They were rough and whiskered; most of them had been drinking; they bellowed, cursed, and shouted coarse jokes.

After five or six minutes, there was a shout, 'Here they come!' and the hubbub died in expectation.

A drum was booming. It faded, then it was close, and a column of men appeared from a side street, marching in time. There were ten of them wearing masks fashioned from neckerchiefs, but the eleventh man, obviously their leader, wore none. He was tall, he had good shoulders, and he carried himself in a manner that indicated a military training.

The whiskered man saw him and knew

that he was the Captain Brass he'd heard about. But that wasn't his real name.

'Cap'n Brass,' he said to one of the miners that were shouldered close against him. 'Funny name, Brass.'

'Likely there ain't fifty men in American Flag know it, but his real name's Brazee. Captain Lon Brazee. He used to be stationed at Fort Ki-whu.'

The whiskered man could have told him that his name wasn't Brazee, either. His real name was Bob Wallace; the 'captain' he'd assumed while touring the Ohio and Mississippi on a showboat as a trick-shot artist. He'd been in the Army, true enough, but they'd drummed him out for stealing government mules after the Mexican campaign. Wallace had hit the trail of '49, and for one reason or another had found it expedient to change his name here and there along the way. In Yuba he'd gone under the name of Simpson, and in Rocky Bar they'd called him Cloyd. At Rocky Bar he'd also headed the vigilantes – strictly for his own profit. There he'd hanged Tincup Joe Horn, calling him a road agent, but the real reason lay in four hundred feet of placer gravel up Tee-mah Gulch.

'Cap'n, hey?' the whiskered man said. 'Well, why ain't he out fighting the war if he's an Army man? Or ain't he got a stomach for Confederate steel?'

'I understand him and the Army had a little misunderstanding over mules.'

'Stole 'em?'

'I'm not damn fool enough to go around saying Captain Brass is a thief. He's not the sort I'd want for an enemy.'

'Ye mean folks hereabout know he's a thief and still they elect him head of their vigilante committee?'

'Hell, you talk like a Pike's Peaker. Nobody pays much attention to a man's ancient history hereabouts. If they did we'd all be taking it down the long coulee.'

Captain Brass marched straight on the crowd, and it gave way. He didn't look to right nor left. He walked straight through and up the seven steps to the platform.

He was in his late thirties, tall and well built. His ramrod spine showed a pride bordering arrogance. He wore a pearl felt hat of a type referred to as a Lone Star; his jacket and trousers were antelope skin rubbed soft and almost white; on his feet were cavalry boots of Spanish leather. It was not an unusual frontier garb, aside from the excellent boots, but Captain Brass had a feel for drama, and he gave it magnificence.

He walked across the platform, coming down hard on his heels, inspected the noose, and left it swinging. He turned with a manner that had once served him on the stage, head back, hands on his hips, and took in the torchlit faces of the crowd with a single, sweeping glance.

He waited while his men ranged themselves below, forming a guard around the platform. While it was going on, the drummer, a grizzled old man no larger than a boy, kept hammering time.

A second group of vigilantes came in sight. They were trying to keep step and make a sort of military show, but the prisoner in their midst gave no co-operation, and they kept breaking time because of him.

At sight of the prisoner a few in the crowd shouted, their voices angry or jeering, but most of the onlookers had became taut-nerved, silenced by the thing they had tried to turn into a celebration.

They brought the man close, and light from the pitch basket fell strongly across his face. He was young, of medium-height, heavy-shouldered. His face was covered by an inch of black whiskers. His hair, long, after the frontier manner, fell in ringlets down his neck. A glisten of perspiration showed along his hairline. They'd bound his arms behind his back, a vigilante was on each side, and, not satisfied with that, a third came behind with a sawed-off shotgun leveled.

They walked him to the gallows steps and stopped while a short, bowed man in a black mask vaulted over the edge and went over to have a look at the noose.

'How is she, Muck?' somebody in the crowd shouted, knowing his identity despite the mask.

Muck turned, and his shoulders jerked back, showing that he'd laughed. 'It'll last a lifetime!'

The grisly joke brought some shouts of laughter, but they were too loud. They were forced. A few minutes before nearly every man there had been merciless in his condemnation of this fellow identified as Comanche John, but it's not easy to hate a man when he stands facing his executioner.

Captain Brass still stood with legs spread a trifle, hands on his hips. He took a deep breath, ready to say something, but the crowd still made too much noise. He waited for silence, and by degrees it came to him. Still he waited. The silence became tense, long-drawn and brittle. It was so quiet one could hear the hurrying thud-thud of a late-comer's boots as he ran up the pole walk, and at a far greater distance the jingle of harness links and the crunch of steel-tired Conestoga freight wagons in tandem finishing the last mile of their long journey up from Salt Lake City.

At last Captain Brass spoke. The black-whiskered man knew what to expect, otherwise the voice would have been a surprise. It was unexpectedly high. Not effeminate. It carried with the treble of finely drawn steel.

'Comanche John!' he said, addressing the prisoner. 'Climb the gallows!'

The prisoner didn't move until a vigilante rammed him hard with his sawed-off shotgun. He stumbled over the bottom step and went to one knee. He got up and the vigilante rammed him again. He climbed the steps then and stood facing Captain Brass.

Brass went on speaking, 'Comanche John, you've received a fair trial. In most camps of Montana Territory you'd have been hanged last night. You'd have been hanged the same hour of your capture. We didn't do that. We gave you every chance to prove yourself innocent. You couldn't do it because you were guilty. The jury found you guilty of robbery and murder, and either charge carries the penalty of death—'

'Hang him twice!' somebody shouted.

Brass ignored him and went on. 'Therefore tonight you will be hanged by the neck until you are dead.'

After speaking these words to the prisoner, he turned and addressed the crowd. 'I guess most of you know what happened well enough, but I'll tell it again because of the false rumors that this man's road-agent friends have been spreading around the camp. Last night the Last Chance coach was held up and robbed. Two of the men on it were killed. One of them was a Dutch harness maker who'd just come to the country.

He didn't even carry a gun. The other was Jack Speer, a miner most of you are acquainted with. Both of those men were shot down without a reason. Just for the love of killing. Because Comanche John hadn't had his man for breakfast. There were six others on the coach – Harry Tigg, Sather, Big-Nose Pierre, Lawson, Gromes the driver, and Shockley the guard. Every man there identified the killer as Comanche John. Last night, this same Comanche John had the gall to ride into town under the noses of us all.'

He turned and pointed a finger at the prisoner. 'And there he is. Comanche John – but the Territory will be rid of him tonight.'

The black-whiskered man muttered, 'Why, the gall o' that dirty road agent! Ain't he got any better manners than ride in hyar under the nose o' that government-mule thief? I say he sure enough deserves to git hung.'

Brass went on in his excellent treble voice, enunciating with a fine precision so the most distant and drunken person in the crowd would not miss a word. 'This man has cut a swath of lawlessness from California all the way to the border of British America, but when he rode into American Flag he made his fatal mistake. The mere fact that he's Comanche John is reason enough to hang him, but we have proof that he robbed the coach and committed murder, too. So no matter what sort of lies they've circulated, now you've heard the *truth*.'

The condemned man had listened, his lips drawn tight, his face turned gaunt and tense. The instant Brass was through, he shouted, 'I'm not Comanche John. *He* knows I'm not. Most of these vigilantes know I'm not. I wasn't near the coach. I can prove where I was if I'm given the chance.'

One of the masked men spun around and drove the back of his hand to the condemned man's jaw. It snapped his head, and he might have fallen if another hadn't been holding him. He was on one knee and he came up again. His mouth was bleeding. Men were shouting, but he could be heard over them.

'I'm not Comanche John, do you hear? I'm not Comanche John! My name's Pike Wilbur. I'm in the freight business. Doesn't that mean anything to you, you fools? I'm in freight business and Brass is in the freight business. That's why he's trying to get me out of the way—'

He'd been shouting and struggling. His arms were tied tightly with elk babiche; there was no freeing them, but he twisted, fought from side to side, and for those seconds he managed to escape the blows that were aimed at him. Then he brought his head up and ran directly into one of the vigilantes' fists.

It was a brutal blow – a short overhand hook. It rocked him and his legs bent. He was on hands and knees. A big vigilante jerked him to his feet.

A raucous voice from the night shouted, 'So you want another chance, John? How much chance did you give Speer and the Dutchman?'

But someone else called out, 'Let him have his say!'

Brass must have realized that the second man represented more of the crowd than the first, because he strode to the gallows' edge and tried to pick his face from the shadow. 'I told you he had a fair trial. He had his chance to speak his piece then. You don't need to think we're going to try him all over again now.'

'Strangler!'

It wasn't loudly spoken, but the word had an edge to it that cut through the babble of lesser speech. Captain Brass heard it and even those at a distance could see the muscles of his arms and shoulders tighten his buckskin shirt. His hands were unquiet. He let them drop, come to rest on the butts of his .44 caliber Army Colts. He took a long, trembly breath. It helped him keep the grip he needed on his temper, then he spoke.

'I heard that. I heard you call me a strangler. I'll overlook it *this* time. I know who said it. I only warn a man once. Next time I'll consider it a *personal* insult and I'll act accordingly.'

He'd kill the next man who called him that. Again there was that dead, taut silence. He let his eyes rove over their heads. Probably he had not one real friend in the camp of American Flag, but even those who hated him most would have to pay him their grudging admiration at that moment. No one there doubted but what he'd fight the crowd singly, or all together if he had to.

Brass was about to go on with the business of hanging when a disturbance at the outer edge of the crowd stopped him. A man was pushing his way toward the gallows. He was skinny and old; he had a straggly gray beard, a rooster neck, an extreme Adam's apple. He wore a black frock coat, and beneath his left arm he was carrying a ratty old Bible.

'There's the Parson!' somebody shouted. 'Can't have a first-class hangin' without the Parson.'

Chapter Two

Gunfire On The Gallows

The Parson managed to claw his way as far as the gallows steps, where the vigilantes stopped him.

'Git out o' my way, ye stranglin' Samaritans o' sin!' he cried in a magpie voice. He swung a wild blow, trying to drive them out of his path, but those who blocked him were young and strong. They flung him away, and he'd have gone flat on his back if the press behind hadn't held him.

'I'm goin' up thar!' he shouted. 'Ye ain't got a right to stop me. Every dyin' man deserves the comfort of a minister o' the cloth.' He called over their heads to Captain Brass. 'But maybe you taken to the idea that you're even greater than the Almighty?'

Brass was irked, but he knew that threats would have no effect on the Parson.

'No man in this camp made a larger contribution toward building that mission house of yours than I did, Parker. You should think of that before saying I have no regard for religion.' He waved at his men and said, 'All right, let him through.'

The Parson wheezed and climbed the steps, saying, 'I'd a' come anyhow. Been a frontier preacher ever since the year o' '42, and no strangler ever kept me from administerin' final solace to a condemned man yet.'

The black-whiskered man grinned and muttered to himself, 'That all may be, Parson, but I *do* seem to recollect a wagon boss that was so bull-headed ye had to convince him with a two-ounce charge o' buck from a squaw gun.'

It was immediately apparent that the

Parson had something on his mind in addition to putting the condemned man at peace with God. He scarcely glanced at the prisoner once he was on the gallows; instead he reared back in a posture not unlike the fighting stance of a game rooster and addressed Captain Brass.

'That man yonder ain't Comanche John. I *know* Comanche John. I've known that black-whiskered sinner for nigh onto seven year. I made a Christian out o' him once, and if it's true he's gone back to his evil habits of coach robbin', by grab I'll make a Christian out o' him again even if I have to bore holes through him with a Navy Colt.'

'H'ray for the Parson!' a drunk shouted.

The Parson was just getting steamed up. He turned his back on Brass and shouted to the crowd, 'I tell ye that man ain't Comanche John! Furthermore, I'm willing to bet gold off the riffle against worthless Yankee greenbacks that he didn't commit that coach robbery and murder, either. And no more did Comanche John. Y'hear that? *Neither of 'em!*'

The Parson had started something now. Everyone seemed to be shouting at once. A big, rawboned fellow charged forward flinging lesser men from his way.

'I seen him!' he roared. 'I seen him, d'you hear me? I was on that coach myself, and I seen him!'

He got to the platform's edge, but the stairs

were blocked by the crowd, and he had to chin himself and belly over. He got to his feet, waved his arms, and stamped his heavy riding-boots with the manners of a braying jackass.

'I seen him kill those men, do you hear that, you Bible-shoutin' old buzzard? I seen him. I seen him and I heard his voice. I seen him shoot Speer and the Dutchman. Shot 'em down like hawgs in the bottoms without givin' 'em a chance. And 'twasn't just me. Sather seen him, too. And so did Big-Nose Pierre. So did–'

'Never mind about it, Tigg,' Brass said. 'We've gone over all this before. We covered every inch of it at the trial, and there's no point in covering it all again. They're just trying to kill time.' His lips were pulled tight, and his voice was brittle, showing the hard effort he was making to restrain his fury. He said to the Parson, 'If you came up here to administer spiritual comfort, get on with it. I'll give you exactly one minute.' He drew out a large gold watch to emphasize that he meant it. 'One minute. If you delay after that time has expired, I'm perfectly capable of having you carried off to jail.'

A girl's voice rose above the noise of the crowd. 'Just a moment, Captain Brass.'

She wasn't the type of girl one usually saw in those wild gold camps, and the men made way for her, letting her go forward.

'It's Faro's daughter,' somebody said.

'Send her home. A hangin's no place for a woman.'

But nobody tried to stop her. Light from the pitch basket struck her as she approached. She was twenty or twenty-one, bronze-haired and extremely pretty. No one could mistake her for one of the painted women who followed the frontier up from California, and yet there was something about her manner which showed that she knew her way among the rough bunch as well as the worst of them. She wasn't afraid of ramming those sweaty, bewhiskered miners, or of elbowing them out of her way if need be. Around her waist was a silvermounted side-hammer pistol, and though she never laid her hand on its stock, something about her way of carrying it served as a warning.

'Dallas!' Captain Brass walked to the edge of the platform and called her by name. 'Dallas, a hanging is no place for a woman like you.'

'It's a place for a woman or anyone who wants to see people get a square deal.'

'Take her away from here,' he said to one of the masked vigilantes.

The man reached for her arm, but she pulled away from him. 'Keep away from me!' The crowd stopped her from putting more than a couple of yards of distance between them, but she faced him with her right hand resting on the pistol, and the vigilante stopped. Even with Brass glaring down at him he didn't want to run the risk of a close-range bullet.

Brass said with grudging admiration, 'Going to fight us all?'

'I have something to say to the people of American Flag!'

'You should have said it at the trial.'

'I'll say it now! That man isn't Comanche John. There are ten men in this camp who have seen Comanche John one time or another in Idaho or down in California. Any of them will swear he's not the one. They would at the trial if they'd been given the chance. But you didn't. The only ones you'd listen to were those so-called *witnesses* you'd loaded the coach with. Then you found him carrying a parfleche bag and used that as some sort of evidence. Why, there are a hundred parfleche bags like that in the country. A handful of rifle ball will buy you one in any Blackfoot lodge between here and the Bear Paws.'

'Take her away!' Brass snarled to the vigilante.

One of them had maneuvered close up behind her. She sensed him and spun. Her hand came up from the holster, and the pistol made a bright shine in the pitchlight. Men scrambled and fell over one another getting out of the line of fire. She backed a step, and the vigilante grabbed her wrist from behind and forced her hands down. The gun exploded, sending flame and bullet beneath the gallows. She fought with twisting, feline strength and almost slipped away before his heavy strength asserted itself. He bent her hand farther and farther down. Her fingers were forced open. The gun dangled for a second, then it fell to the ground.

'Sorry, Dallas,' Brass said. She was helpless now, so he pretended to be sorry for her. 'You'll think about this tomorrow and know I'm right.'

'It's a deadfall!' the Parson screamed. 'Ye hear me? It's a deadfall of the devil.'

He walked towards Captain Brass. As he drew near, he lifted the Bible and a clenched fist overhead. His gray beard and wild, protruding eyeballs made him resemble some avenging prophet from the pages of the Old Testament. 'Ye strangler You and your coward crew that hangs men, by night without even the bravery to show your faces! Behold my words, there's a special pit o' hell for the kind o' men that use what they call *the law* to kill for special advantage. You with your make-believe trial and your masked band of stranglers that calls itself a vigilante committee–'

Captain Brass moved suddenly. His arm shot out; his hand closed on the Parson's skinny neck. It was a powerful hand, and it crushed the remainder of the old man's sentence in his windpipe.

The Parson writhed from side to side. He clawed at Brass's fingers, but they were powerful as a steel clamp.

Brass took a step, another. The Parson's knees buckled. He'd have fallen if Brass hadn't been holding him. Then Brass shook him. He snapped him back and forth with his old gray head flopping loose, with his hair stringing across his face.

A gun crashed, and Brass sprang back, letting go his hold. He made a clutch at his wrist. A bullet had struck him there. Blood was running through his fingers.

He seemed to be momentarily stunned, and so was the crowd. For the instant no one knew where the shot came from. The Parson had gone face down to the gallows planks. He pulled himself to hands and knees with his gray hair caught in the splinters. He looked around, and his eyes came to focus on the black-whiskered man just vaulting over the edge.

The Parson's lips formed the word 'John', but the whiskered man said, 'Stay down, ye old pelican!'

The whiskered man then stood in the full light of the pitch basket. He was slouched, apparently careless in dusty jackboots and wrinkled homespuns. He held a Navy Colt in each hand, and a wisp of powder smoke still curled from the muzzle of one of them.

He tilted his head at the condemned man and spat tobacco juice. 'Parson's right. He ain't Comanche John, and that's the truth. I know he ain't, because I'm Comanche John myself.'

A moment of silence followed his astonishing admission. Then, from the back of the crowd, rose the voice of White-Eyes, the blind man.

'That's him! I never forget a voice. That's Comanche John. It's the old ring-tailed ripper himself. Toughest, roughest, war-whooping gun talker that ever beat hair off a horse on the long trail from Californy. Look at him, brothers, and give him room, because I'd just as soon do battle with a bar'l of rattlesnakes.'

John said, 'White-Eyes, that's all true for a fact. Why don't ye sing 'em the song about me shootin' up the town o' Rocky Bar?'

From beneath the black slouch hat, Comanche John's eyes kept roving the edge of the crowd, watching the masked vigilantes. All of them were well-armed, most of them with sawed-off guns in addition to the usual Navy Colts, but surprise had momentarily frozen them, and now, beneath his narrow gaze, not one was willing to make the first move.

'What's wrong, ye stranglers? Are ye scairt to show the muzzles o' your guns just like you're scairt to show your faces? I only got eleven shots left. Thirteen including the two in my derringer. Whichever o' you woolly wolves happens to be number fourteen, why I'm his meat.'

John spattered a stream of tobacco juice. He wasn't pointing his guns, just holding them, dangling at the ends of his long arms. Outnumbered as he was it seemed ridiculous that he'd hold them off, but his reputation was ominous, and those masked vigilantes had come to put on a nice, safe hanging and not get a bellyful of bullet lead.

Tigg, the rawboned man who had given his 'eyewitness' account, edged back until he was hidden by one of the vigilantes. There he felt safe enough to draw the gun from his right-hand holster. He lifted it slowly, careful to move nothing but his forearm. With the revolver's long barrel clear he moved into the open, but John had been watching him. The Navy in his left hand came to life with explosion and a streak of flame, and Tigg went down.

'Right betwixt the eyes,' John said. 'Don't be bashful, boys, just step right up and take your turn. Can't ever tell, White-Eyes yonder might even put your names in a new verse of my song, and thar you'd be, famous.'

The Parson had staggered to his feet. His cheek was bleeding. He kept fingering his hair and getting blood mixed with it. He'd been trying to talk for the last twenty or thirty seconds, but his mouth merely opened and closed like a chicken in need of water.

Now he said in his hoarse cackle, 'John, I knew ye'd come. I knew ye'd come riding in here and scatter this buzzard crew. I knew Comanche John wouldn't let any pore young pilgrim get rope-stretched in his name.'

'Cut him loose, ye old Bible shouter before all three of us git hung.' He said it from the side of his mouth, never letting his eyes leave the crowd. Brass was on one knee, still holding his wrist. Blood kept running, dripping off the tips of his fingers. No longer were his eyes off-focus from bullet shock. He was the old Captain Brass, not beaten, just recognizing the momentary percentages and making no move for the guns at his hips.

'Ye damned, dumb Yankees,' John said. 'Even a bunch o' Pike's Peakers and abolitionists ought to see through a deadfall like this'n. It war a frame-up – robbery and everything – a frame-up. Nobody got robbed last night. Unless maybe those two men that got kilt. Way it looks, maybe they were the only two honest men aboard. That'd be reason to shoot 'em – so's they couldn't testify. How about it, Brass? You have some private reason to hang this poor pilgrim? Whar you made your mistake was trying to make out he was me.'

The Parson had cut him loose, and now, with him standing beside the real Comanche John, it could be seen there was scarcely any similarity between them, except that both were stockily built and both had faces covered by an inch of dark beard.

John moved to the back of the platform. His right-hand Navy was tilted, aimed at the pitch basket chain. He fired, cut the chain, and the basket fell. It narrowly missed the edge of the platform and struck the ground, flinging blazing pitch and shavings over a ten-foot area. The light was brighter than before, but it was on the earth, leaving the gallows platform in shadow.

The crowd was by no means against the vigilantes, and a good many men out there had been waiting their first chance to go for their guns.

The chance was now. Guns ripped from half a dozen directions, their explosions almost in unison.

Comanche John was no longer in sight on the gallows. There was a stampede as a hundred men rushed forward. Over the tumult rose the clear, high tones of Captain Brass's voice.

'Here he is, flat on the gallows!'

Brass opened fire with both pistols, but he had too much respect for the marksmanship of Comanche John, and his own aim was spoiled as John rolled toward the edge.

John had anticipated the volley that would follow his shooting the pitch basket. He'd gone face foremost, felt the roar of pistol balls passing over him. He rolled over and over;

40

paused on one elbow to exchange bullets with Brass. The advantage of darkness was also a handicap, and his slug merely tore splinters from the post by the Captain's side.

Next second Brass went over the edge. He turned, agile as a bobcat, and landed on his feet. He was bent over, using the edge for protection. He ran three steps, bobbed up unexpectedly, and his guns crashed three times, aiming at John's position as it had been revealed by powder flame a second before. But John was no longer there, and the bullets, ripping across the platform, served only to send his own men scrambling for cover.

John had rolled over again and lunged to his feet. The scaffold upright was a momentary protection. He could see the hangrope with its heavy noose dangling at one side of him. He took three running steps and seized the noose. The rope swung him out and away. He sensed the instant of his greatest arch and let go. Momentarily he was over their heads, silhouetted against the night sky. He alighted on the pole awning of the Gold City Saloon.

The poles had been laid flat, notched to fit, but held without nails. One of them rolled underfoot. He made a blind grab and saved himself by means of some elk horns that had been fastened to the saloon's false front.

A blast of buckshot whipped the night. Both barrels of an eight-gauge. He was moving, and the charge splintered a plank of the false front at his shoulder.

He seized the top log. It was high. He chinned himself, pulled himself over, fell to the steep gable of the roof. He grabbed hold and took a second or two to look around.

He could have slid down the roof and been safe for the moment, but there was too great a chance of being trapped. Next door was an assayer's shop, and after that the two-story White Palace gambling-house, several shanties housing saloons and stores, and the washee where his gunpowder roan was tied.

He clambered along the gable. For an instant he was visible, and guns roared in a volley, but he was gone from sight down the steep shake roof.

He dug in his boot heels to check himself and rocked to his feet in time to take two running steps and leap to the assayer's roof, a distance of ten feet.

It was a low roof, almost flat, made of planks covered by dirt and gravel.

'He's there on the assay shop!' he could hear Brass shout. 'The assayer's, you damned fools—'

A high chimney from the furnace gave him protection while he climbed through one of the open windows of the White Palace's second story.

He was in a small bedroom. It seemed hot. He stayed on one knee while getting his breath; then, after ten or fifteen seconds he groped along the wall, found the door stepped into a hall. Light came from the well of a stairway, but the big gambling-house seemed to be empty. He crossed to another room, dropped from its window to the roof below, and crossed other buildings to the washee where the gunpowder was still waiting.

The horse snorted and jerked back on the bridle reins when Comanche John dropped beside him, but he subsided with scarcely a flank quiver at sound of the man's easy voice.

'Sure, Gunpowder. Sure, boy. It's only a bit o' shooting and nothing so strange about that, boy.'

He pulled the reins free and mounted. Boots made a steady rumble along the pole walks, and someone was riding at a gallop, clattering stones in the street. In another minute they'd be combing every alley in town.

As he rode off he could hear White-Eyes singing in a wild, challenging voice:

'Co-man-che John rode to I-dee-ho
In the year of 'sixty-three,
With a pal named Whiskey Anderson
A gunman from Mo-hee,
Two straighter shootin' highwaymen

Ye seldom ever knew,
Oh listen to my stor-ee
I'll tell ye what they do–'

Chapter Three

Just A Pore Pilgrim

The gunpowder roan seemed to know what was expected of him. Comanche John merely nudged him with one knee, gave him his head, and the horse picked his way rapidly around heaps of bottles, then in and out among cabins to the outskirts of the town.

He could hear men shouting, with now and then a pistol shot. Horsemen kept appearing from the dark, riding hard, headed toward the mountain trails. Brass was sending them out there, not on a blind chase, but to lie low in hopes of getting him from ambush.

The deep gash of a placer mine blocked his way, and he drew up at its precipitous edge wondering which way to turn. He gave the appearance of having unlimited time at his disposal. Below by the light of pitch torches, he could see Chinese carrying gravel, coolie-fashion, in baskets on spring poles, paying no heed to the events ripping apart the white man's world topside. The mine, one of the camp's original discoveries and already worked out according to American standards, was still a good thing for the Orientals, and they'd keep scratching away at it in their anthill manner for years, washing out a dollar or two a day.

He reloaded his Navies, taking his time, inspecting them twice before returning them to the holsters. He even freshened his chaw of tobacco, then he turned and followed the placer mine for half a mile to the lower end of town.

He came to some corrals and a pole shed. No one was around. He turned the gunpowder roan inside the gate with a greenback tied to one of the saddle strings for the hostler then he struck through the outskirt cabins and found the back door of the Parson's mission.

He listened a few seconds with his ear against the door planks. No sound. No light coming from the cracks around it. He pulled the latch, the door opened, he went inside, stood for a moment, spoke.

'Parson!'

He got no answer and he'd expected none. Not even Brass would think of laying an ambush there. His eyes grew used to the deeper darkness, and the windows became visible. They weren't of glass. These were the parchment windows of the frontier-deer hide, scraped, oiled, and turned translucent by the semi-arid climate. No one could see through them, even though a light burned inside, so he fumbled around the table and found flint, steel, and tinder. A minute later he had a spark burning and lighted the wick of a tallow-dip lamp.

He could see the mission then. It was a single, long room, furnished with plank benches. Banners, painted in trade vermilion, were hung along the walls: *Vengeance Is Mine Saith the Lord. Will Your Mother Find Ye There? Will Ye Be Caught On the Riffles of Heaven or Washed Down the Tailings to Hell?* The banners were familiar to John, and he'd seen them elsewhere, at the mission in Rocky Bar, and at Bannack before that.

There was a platform, and on it a pulpit of whipsawed plank. Shelves beneath were stacked full of hymnals. He looked at one, blue, with its front illustrated by silver angels who were far from home in that town of American Flag. A curtain shut off the corner of the room where the Parson slept.

John put down the lamp, seated himself in the Parson's willow easy chair, and histed his jackboots. He dozed off, but he was instantly awake when someone pulled the latch of the front door.

He'd placed himself in the shadows, and he sat quite still, his eyes fastened on the door, his jaw not even revolving around tobacco. It was the Parson, all right, and there was a man with him – that dark-bearded young fellow who had so recently stood on the vigilante gallows.

The Parson closed the door and looked the room twice over before he made out the form of Comanche John back in the shadow.

'So it is you! I reckoned it'd be when I seen the light. "The oceans o' the world may chaw away at the land until the face of a continent changes, but a danged fool stays the same for ever and ever." That's from the Greenwood fourth reader, and truer words were never penned. I said to myself, "He'll be fool enough to come here," and sure enough, here ye be. If you ain't got regard for your own unwashed hide, ye might have for the good name o' my mission.'

'I been washed in the blood o' the lamb,' said John.

'Ye been washed in the blood of iniquity, and your gullet's corroded with the wages of sin. How'd it look to folks here in American Flag if they found out I harboured road agents?'

'Share and share alike's my motto. That's my own, personal golden rule, Parson. I'm just a pore pilgrim come in out o' the blackness of night, hankering for spiritual guidance.'

'You're a highway robber on the jump from every sheriff's posse and vigilante committee betwixt here and Sacramento.'

'I've ranged plenty farther'n Sacramento, Parson. Anyhow, you ain't doing me justice. If you'd quit psalm singin' for a while and give an ear to some of the tunes the year o' '64, you'd find out that everybody don't hold me in so low regard. Not by a jugful they don't. Why, I'm one of the most sought-after men in this territory.'

'John, it's unsafe here. They're out to get you, them stranglers. They'll shoot on sight. They'll drill gun holes through ye till you leak like a funnel.'

'I reckon you'll get Providence on my side, Parson, so I'll be safe enough for tonight.' He shook hands with both of them, with the Parson warmly, after the manner of one renewing an old friendship, and with the young men, whose name was Pike Wilbur, using a long grab and keeping his left hand free. John's years along the back trails had taught him never to trust anybody. Even this young Pike Wilbur, whom he'd just saved from the noose could be one of the detectives hired by Ben Holladay.

He sat back down and inspected the loads in his Navy Colts. 'I can see you'd never make a success as a road agent, Parson. Now this thing o' hidin' out, for instance. Best place to hide is somewhere that's so damned foolish nobody'd think of it. Mind one night, about a month ago, down in Yallerjack. That's one o' those I-dee-ho camps, you know, and you can't beat 'em for downright cussedness. I was peaceful, with nothing on my mind but good fellow-ship and a few snorts of trade likker at a saloon, when somebody let out a yip, sayin', "Thar's Comanche John!"

'Waal, Yallerjack ain't a big camp, and it don't get famous men like me every day of the week, so there was a lot of excitement, and pretty soon somebody got the idee o' giving me a party to celebrate. Wanted to give me a present, too. Think it was a cravat. Not only that, they had it in mind to tie the knot themselves and have me entertain with a solo jig right after they got it on me. So I says, "Hold on, you keep your blasted cravat and give it to somebody hankerin' for such," and I lit out with the whole camp hot on my trail.

'I didn't get much of a jump, and it was nip and tuck for a while with maybe just a bit more nip than tuck, so I circled around and put Gunpowder up in the jail stable and gave him a bucketful of the sheriff's oats, and then, not having a better place to go, I went inside the sheriff's cabin and crawled into his bed, him being a bachelor and lonesome.

'The sheriff wasn't thar right then, o' course, but he came in sometime late and crawled in beside me. "Who be ye?" he asks. "Ought to know who I be," says I. "Be ye Buck?" and I says, "Buck I be." Waal, I got up along before dawn and put on my clothes, but it was dark, and by the purest accident I just happened to put on his new pants instead of my old ones.' John stood up and turned around, displaying his substantial homespuns for the Parson to admire. 'Everything considered, they turned out to be a fair fit.'

While the Parson got a fire going beneath a pot of venison stew, John talked to Pike Wilbur.

'You got yourself in a tight one. Could be you're acquainted with Cap'n Brass from someplace else? He has a way o' getting vigilante committees together to settle his old scores.'

'I never met him before. I came upriver from St Louis and I guess he got here by way of California.'

'You mean *Californy?*'

'Californy,' said Pike Wilbur.

On the scaffold he looked like he might be in his late twenties or early thirties, but now, smiling, there was something boyish about him that couldn't be covered by his growth of whiskers. He was about twenty-three.

While waiting to eat, Pike told about himself, how with his father he'd run freight wagons between Independence, Missouri, and Santa Fe and how after his father's death he'd refloated a steamboat sunk by the Confederate troops near Cape Girardeau and run the Missouri blockade between

50

there and Fort Leavenworth.

John stopped chewing and said, 'You mean to say you're on the side o' the North?'

'Don't bring the rebellion in here!' the Parson said. 'Seems to me the two of you got plenty of fightin' to do in Montana Territory without dragging Jeff Davis and Abe Lincoln into the picture.'

Pike Wilbur went on with his story, telling how the steamboat had made him a small stake until it was captured and burned by Quantrell's bushrangers near Bow Island. When that happened he set out upriver in search of opportunities.

Fort Benton he found to be booming. This former fort of the Chouteau Fur Company was at the end of river navigation on the Missouri. There, blocked by swift water and the Great Falls, freight for the fabulously rich gold camps of the Montana Rockies was taken ashore, reloaded on wagons, and sent by jerk-line mule and ox outfits across prairie and mountains from two hundred to four hundred miles. However, he found that the falls blocked navigation for scarcely twenty miles, after which a smaller boat of light draft could operate all the way to American Flag. So, working quietly not to alarm the interests making fortunes from horse-drawn freight, he'd started building the hull, and he'd ordered a small engine and boiler from the Richardson works in St

Louis. However, his purpose became known, and competition quickly developed.

'Cap'n Brass?' John asked. 'So that's why he had his noose out for ye! He didn't want anybody breaking up that nice, tight freight monopoly he's got betwixt hyar and Benton.'

'I played into his hands. I should have come here openly, admitting who I was.'

'Why, that's open to question, too. Fellows like Brass are tough to go up agin' no matter how you do it. What was the truth of that robbery and killin' he tried to hang on you?'

'You know as much about it as I do. They said the coach was robbed and two men were killed, and pretty soon those fellows started to identify me.'

The Parson said, 'Closest I can figure it, Jack Speer was aboard that coach with a big roll of greenbacks in his satchel, so them varmints o' Brass's decided they might as well get two chickens with one shot. So they robbed him and kilt him together with that Dutchman, then they all swore it was Pike. Where they went too far was claiming Pike was really Comanche John. I suppose Brass did it so nobody would oppose the hanging. Wanted to make a hero of himself, too. Only as it turned out, thar was too many knew *that* varmint from Californy.'

John said to Pike, 'Who tipped Brass off you were here?'

'The only man I knew in this camp was

Faro Hill, owner of the White Palace—'

'He's dead,' said the Parson. 'Shot dead. Couple of months ago. Nobody knows who did it. Honest folk don't, anyhow. That gal, Dallas, has been running the White Palace since then, and you can bet your Navies *she* didn't give the information.'

The Parson served strong green tea, venison stew, and cold bannock. Things had quietened down outside. There were just the usual sounds of the camp now – the steady clump and talk of men, music and laughter from dance halls, the distant clatter of freight outfits completing their long drag from Benton or Salt Lake.

The men had about completed their meal when the front door opened and a girl spoke. It was Dallas Hill.

'Parson!'

'Yes, Miss Dallas. You come on in.'

She closed the door. Her moccasins made scarcely a whisper across the heavy plank floor. She saw Pike Wilbur and said, 'You're still here!' Her voice sounded relieved.

'All right, John,' the Parson said, trying to see him overhead, among the rafters. 'Ye can come down now. She's by herself.'

Comanche John lowered himself with an easy strength, and dropped to the floor. Dallas Hill started back from surprise.

'I thought you'd left town long ago.'

'Without my supper, child?'

53

'They're looking for you everywhere–'

'Ain't looked hyar. Fetched if I can understand why. Verse in my song says I'm a converted Christian o' the Parson's.'

'They know what your horse looks like. A boy saw you ride into camp. If you have him tied somewhere out behind–'

'Got him in that livery corral, back yonder by the Chinese diggin's.'

'That corral belongs to Captain Brass's freight line.'

John did a fandango dance on his jackboots, slapping dust from his homespuns with delight. 'Why, that's rich. That's nigh perfect. Bless me, Parson, if this ain't gettin' nigh onto as good as Yallerjack.'

She was still concerned. 'It's nothing to joke about. You don't understand how powerful he is here in American Flag. Those men may curse him behind his back and call him a strangler, but they trust him, and they believe he's saved the camp from being easy prey for road agents like Virginia and Confederate Gulch were. He'll hang you if he–'

'Now, child. Don't you go worrying about the old Comanche. He's been chased by vigilantes in Californy, and he's chased by 'em in I-dee-ho, and he ain't stretched rope yet. The old Comanche dies hard. So you just sit easy and tell what you came to tell.'

She said to Pike, 'My father had a share in that boat you're building up by the Great

54

Falls, didn't he?'

'Yes. It was his idea. I talked to him last year in Fort Leavenworth. I didn't know he'd been killed till I came to town. Then I tried to find you.'

'I know. I thought it would be better if Brass didn't find out. I have to keep the White Palace going. He could make it tough on me.'

John said, 'Now that's something ye forgot to mention – Faro Hill being in on your boat. What'd he do, stake ye to part of the cost when ye seen him at Leavenworth?'

'Yes. We were fifty-fifty partners. Faro's share falls to Dallas, so that makes her my partner. If she wants to be.'

'Could be,' said John, 'that Cap'n Brass found out about it two months ago. Could be that's why Faro got that bullet lead in the back.'

She said, 'Of course that's why he was killed. The one who controls the transportation into this country is the one who'll make the big fortune once the quartz lodes are tapped. Dad said these placers were only the white chips. The real stakes, the blue chips, are the lodes bearing silver, gold, and copper back in the mountains. It's more than just hauling the black-eyed beans to supply this camp. Brass wants to control the river. If he can't stop you from building, he'll build a boat of his own.'

'But we'll be *first!*' Pike Wilbur struck the table with his fist, making the tin dishes dance. 'We'll be first, and we'll make the mail contract and the gold contracts with the St Louis banks because we *are* first.'

John said, 'Now, now, children. Seems to me you're pickin' the hard way. Why'nt I just amble over yonder and put a couple o' Navy slugs through this Cap'n Brass, and we'll have him all took care of, neat and permanent. It'd be simple, and it'd be a task I'd enjoy. I had a little score to settle with that gentleman when I rode into camp, anyhow. Ye see, he hung a partner o' mine over at Rocky Bar.'

She said, 'No, John. It won't do. You're in danger here. You'd better drift.'

'Why, child, I wouldn't–'

'She's tryin' to say it wouldn't help 'em any to get tied up with a dirty, low, ornery road agent,' the Parson said. 'Best way you can help these young folk is by clearin' out. If Brass could tie you up with that boat he'd have a good legal excuse to ride over yonder with his vigilantes. Maybe he'd talk the Benton vigilante committee to take a hand, too. John, she's right. It'd be better for everybody if you just lit out.'

John looked around. Pike Wilbur met his eyes for a second. Nothing was said. It wasn't easy for Pike, owing his life to Comanche John and having to admit that the

56

Parson had spoken the truth.

'Why, I guess maybe you're right.' John speared the last piece of venison on his bowie, then he carefully wiped the blade on a bit of bannock and put it away in its scabbard. He stood up. 'Best thing I can do is drift. Best thing for you, and the best thing for myself. Never saw it fail; a man in my line o' business lets grass grow under his boots and next thing anybody knows it's growin' atop him. This upper Missouri country's gettin' too damn full o' Yankees to suit me, anyhow.'

The Parson said, 'John, I don't want to hear that you gone back to robbin' coaches.'

'*Me?* Parson, all I ask is the chance o' helpin' the weary pilgrim on his way. Share and share alike's my motto. That's Christian, Parson. That's proof that all the missionary work you done on me ain't been in vain.'

Chapter Four

Strong Smell O' Rattler

Comanche John blew out the grease dip. He opened the door without showing himself, hesitated a second or two, and moved outside, closing the door after him. There was a bright moon, but the rear of the mission was in heavy shadow. He took time to gnaw off a fresh cheekful of tobacco. Nothing suspicious. Everything quiet just the usual sounds of saloons and dance halls. Still he did not cross directly to the corral, but circled and came up to it from the downhill side.

Candlelight came through the open door of a shed, and he could see a man's shadow as he moved around inside. No voices. Evidently the man was alone. John kept walking, slouched and careless, and stopped to look inside. The man, tall and skinny with a bristly shock of hair, was bent over, pawing through a harness box. Suddenly he realized someone was watching and he spun around.

His expression, the open mouth and protruding eyeballs, told John he'd been recognized. He'd expected that. Scarcely a man in American Flag hadn't been at the hanging.

The fellow remained for a second, too surprised to move. His sharp eyeballs shifted to a Navy pistol that hung in its holster on a peg. It was only arm's reach away, but he didn't try for it. He opened his mouth to speak, and after a couple of tries some words came.

'What in the– You?'

'Yep. Me. Comanche John. But you don't need to be scairt. I already had my man for supper, and breakfast is still a long way off. Tonight I'm shootin' nothing but varmints, so just be careful and don't put yourself in that class, and the two of us will git along like flapjacks and sorghum.'

'I'm peaceful. I ain't gettin' paid to swap lead with anybody. I'm just a poor damn hay shoveler. I don't have any truck with vigilante stranglers anyhow.'

John moved inside. An ornate saddle of Spanish-tooled leather decorated with hammered silver hung on a peg. From the looks of it, it had just been cleaned and polished.

'Be they a Mexican general hereabouts?'

'You mean the saddle? That's Captain Brass's saddle. He owns this spread. He—'

'So I been told, but I ain't interested in Cap'n Brass, I'm interested in me. You fetch that saddle, and then we'll see about a horse fitten for my station in life.'

He chose a fine chestnut gelding and watched it being saddled. He mounted, said, 'You stay thar,' to the hostler, and set off at an easy jog with Gunpowder on a lead string behind.

After a hundred yards some cabins hid him, and immediately he heard the hostler shouting, 'I saw him! Comanche John! He was here. He stole a couple o' horses and headed that way, toward the Chinee diggin's.'

John kicked his horse to a gallop. He weaved among some outskirt cabins. The mountain lay beyond. It steepened. There was a fork in the trail. One branch led to the

Benton stage road, the other to some hard-rock mining locations on the higher slopes.

He turned toward the mines. In that direction the trail would fork again and again, dissipating his pursuit.

Someone sighted him, shouted, 'Thar he goes!' and fired.

A gun was a distant streak of flame. The bullet struck rocks thirty yards at his heels and whined away. Then he found the welcome cover of some lodgepole timber.

He slowed and watched for a side trail. Finding none, he turned directly up the mountain, hunting a way across rock and windfalls.

It got steeper, so he dismounted and went ahead, leading the horses. After ten minutes he stopped to listen. Hoofs were on the gallop, but echo made their direction uncertain.

He reached the base of a cliff, turned along it, and followed a game trail that wound around through heaps of slab porphyry and at last took him to the mountain crest.

He stopped there to get his breath. The river was a bright strip of reflection between black-timbered mountains. American Flag, far below, was shrunken, a scattering of lights, insignificant.

He grunted, 'Yankee camp!' and spat. He was through with it. But not through with Brass. Someday he'd run into that one again.

There were riders, five of them in a line,

pushing hard up one of the trails.

'Best we go, hoss,' he said. 'Wouldn't want to get caught in any cross fires. Not twice in one night.'

He dropped from the crest down a series of mountain terraces, then low ground with beaver meadows. The gulch narrowed, he followed a stream, and after another hour of travel reached the Missouri.

The river here was swift and cold so clear that even by moonlight he could see the rocks along its bottom. Not for another hundred miles, until its confluence with the Sun, would it deserve the name 'Big Muddy'. He followed a trail along its marge for three miles and forded some gravel-bottomed shallows.

Wild country now. A man had to be wary of Blackfoot war parties. Wary, too, of prospectors who were likely to get trigger-itchy if they suspected someone of snooping around their diggings. He'd never traveled the country before, but its mountain landmarks were familiar to him, and he knew where he was going. A day's travel to the west was the robbers' roost camp of Piegan City. There he'd be able to hide out for a couple of weeks, to rest his bones and let the gunpowder put some fat on. It might not be healthy riding down toward Last Chance or Confederate Gulch after that ruckus in American Flag.

The sun came up, and it felt good on his back after the long cold of mountain night.

He kept going, letting the bay take his own speed until late morning, then he shot a grouse, roasted it on a stick, and ate it Injun-style without salt. He unsaddled and let the horses graze. No pursuit that he could see. Toward evening he rode on.

The trail angled north toward a mountain pass used by the explorers Lewis and Clark a little more than half a century before. Mountains there were sharper, the gulches grading into canyons. Far below he could see some flats, a cluster of cabins, and a thin spiral of wood smoke. That was Piegan City, a placer camp until its rich gravel had been exhausted, and now, abandoned by miners, it had become a robbers' roost, a hide-out for road agents, Army deserters, renegades.

He started downhill, following a switchback trail that took him through miles of timber. It was an hour later and growing dark when he reached the bottom and rode across flats that were scarred by placer trenches. Here and there, through scrub timber, he could see the parchment windows of cabins, yellow-glowing with candlelight behind them.

A skinny black-and-tan dog darted out to bark, spiteful and insistent. There was a corral, and a dozen horses with their heads hung over the top rail, looking at him. No sign of men, but he knew that someone would be watching. Piegan City wasn't the sort of place a man took by surprise.

He swung down and watered his horses at the little clear-cold brook. There was movement behind him, and the sharp *click* as a gun hammer was drawn to cock.

'Waal, now, so ye got me covered!' he drawled without turning.

'You're covered, all right,' a man answered in nasal voice. He was about twenty steps off, in the black shadow beyond a shed. 'Don't try anything, stranger, because the trigger catch on this old smokehouse is nigh wore out so she goes off when I breathe too heavy. What you looking for here at Piegan?'

'Just for a chance to rest my tired bones till the vigilantes get off my trail.'

'*What* vigilantes?'

'Why, all the vigilantes. Clean from here to Yuba City, if ye want the truth of it.'

'Then you must be a curly wolf for sure. Must be you're even *worse'n* Comanche John.'

'They aint' nobody worse'n Comanche John. I know because I *be* Comanche John.'

'Yes, and I be Maximilian, emperor of Mexico.'

John turned slowly, thumbs hooked in the band of his homespuns just over the Navy Colts, and saw the man standing beyond the corner of the shed. He was a gangling scarecrow with one side of his face drawn out of shape by a huge chaw of tobacco. He held a Navy in his right hand, cocked and pointed. John regarded him, grunted, and spattered a stream of tobacco juice almost to the toes of his boots.

'Why, you dumb Yankee, o' course I'm Comanche John. I could o' kilt you already when I first seen ye creepin' around the shed before the horses was watered. What's wrong hyar in Piegan City, givin' this sort o' welcome to a pilgrim with vigilantes on his trail?'

'Put up your gun, Rambo!' a man said, and John recognized his voice. It was Shep Shepherd, a killer and renegade who'd once been with the old Pistol Rock gang operating along the freight road between Lewiston and Walla Walla. He ambled forward, tall and slope-shouldered, red-whiskered, an utterly shapeless hat on the back of his head. Apparently he never changed his clothes, day or night, until they fell off him; and they were reaching that state now. Around his lean hips hung a brace of pistols – not Navies, but Army forty-fours, the sort that used the new metallic ammunition. He'd seen an identical pair on Captain Brass at American Flag.

Rambo turned to Shep and said, 'This old wolf claims that he's Comanche John–'

'And so he be, you ignorant Pike County punkin roller.'

Rambo gulped and almost swallowed his chaw of tobacco. Even in the twilight John could see his color change. He was suddenly sick-scared. He gripped his gun so hard it trembled, and he had to make three jabs at his holster before putting it away.

John drawled, 'Ye see? See how close-comin' ye got to that three-seven-seventy-seven hole in the ground the vigilantes are always talkin' about.'

There was movement here and there in the dark as men came up from the cabins, but none of them got close except Shepherd.

He stood, grinning, and said, 'Yep, it's the old Comanche!' He was proud that he knew Comanche John. He thought everyone was admiring him, that it put him in John's class, a real ring-tailed roarer. 'Mind the old days when we hung out in the Snake River country?'

'I remember 'em.' John shook hands with Shep like he'd shake with any man, but there was no friendship in it. The gaze he fastened on him was one he might have given a puff adder.

'You must recollect me, then. I was with the old Pistol Rock gang. Mind that night in Orofino when–'

'Sure, I recollect. You're Shep Shepherd. You were with Tatlow when he raided the emigrant train along the cliffs at Bird Tail Pass. Run the wagons overside, and shot men down without giving 'em a chance. Now there was a low-varmint piece o'business.'

For a few seconds, Shep's face was mean and truculent, then he decided to treat it as a joke.

'John, you're still ornery as a center-sprung buzz saw. But anyhow, let's not have the skunk telling the polecat how stink'n' he smells, because I hear plenty bad stories about you, too.'

'Then I guess you went to Rocky Bar and shot a man whilst he was asleep, and ye renegaded it among the Injuns and beat up your squaw until even the Arapahoes couldn't stomach ye.'

Shep bent double with laughter, holding his middle. 'I'm a mean one, all right. I'm meaner'n a rattlesnake in August. I'm a ring-tailed ripper. I drink water out of the crick like a horse. I ain't curried my hair or took a bath since the year of '49, and I still got the same family o' lice I started out from Kaintuck with when I was a boy.'

John left him, still heehawing, unsaddled, hobbled the horses, and turned them loose in the pasture that lay beyond some placer diggings. By that time the last twilight had faded and stars were out. He walked to the big log house. Thirteen or fourteen men were seated on a bench under the pole awning, talking and slapping at mosquitoes. They fell silent when he approached. He stopped, freshened his chaw of tobacco, and passed some ordinary remarks about the evening.

It was his first chance really to judge the crowd. They weren't like the one he'd found at that robbers' roost during a couple of previous visits. Before, they'd been mostly drifters, vagabonds of the gold camps, and army deserters, with a few worse who'd be classed as road agents. These men were more hardened and reticent, and he had a hunch they'd run the others out.

'Shep around?' he asked.

'Inside,' one of them growled.

They all sat watching him, hands close to their pistols as he opened the door and went in.

The cabin was hot from the fireplace, filled with the greasy, rancid smell of frying salt pork. Shep sat with his boots high as his head on the edge of the table and shuffled a ratty deck of cards.

'Come on in,' he said.

'In I be.'

John closed the door. He looked around and saw Rambo cross-legged on the floor in front of the fire, with a tin plate of salt pork and doughgods on his knees, eating with his bowie.

'Have you et?' Shep asked.

'No.'

'Rambo, you fry up some victuals that's fitten for the most famous road agent in the Nor'west.'

Rambo rocked forward and haggled off several half-inch-thick slices of salt pork, laid them in a blackened frying-pan. His

67

back was partly turned, but John knew he was watching from the corner of his eyes.

Shep said, 'Rest your hocks, John, and tell me what sort of hell-raisin' you been up to. Last story I heard you'd got yourself hung down in Virginny City.'

'They hung me in Rawhide, and Yallerjack, and they hung me on the Beaverhead, too.' John deliberately left out mention of American Flag. He'd lone-wolfed it long enough to know it was no more a good idea to tell where he'd been than where he was going.

'Still in the coach business?'

'I do a little o' this and a little o' that.'

'Pretty hard for a man operating all alone these days. The express company's getting smarted up. Always sending out them dummy boxes so a man never knows which coach has the gold on 'er. Getting these days so a man needs somebody planted at the express office or he's likely to get nothing but the passengers' wallets.'

Shep was getting around to something, and John said, 'Could be you have somebody on the inside?'

'Well, I wouldn't say that, but I got some important friends in these Montana camps.'

Shepherd swaggered a little. He stood and took a hitch in his filthy trousers. He was grinning, and that made the chaw of tobacco pull his face even farther out of shape. He wanted John to ask concerning the nature of his influence, but John stretched out his jack-boots and said, 'Waal, such things don't interest me nowadays. Maybe you ain't heered, but I reformed. Took and got religion and I ain't lifted so much as an ounce of the heavy yaller off a coach since Feb'wary. That is, none except a poke or two off that Bannack coach because she was so heavy-loaded I knew she'd never pull the Badger Pass.'

'Only way they'll ever reform you is with a hangrope.'

'No, Shep. I seen the arrers o' my ways. Road-agentin' is a hard life, and the good ye do ye never get credit for. I ain't old, but I'm gettin' along. What I look for now is peace and the quiet life. A good fire under the chimney, a pot o' beans bubblin' on the hook, and maybe a Blackfoot squaw to putter around and sew my clothes for me – that's what a man craves when he gets my age. I thought it over for a spell now, and I about decided to retire and let the younger men take over.'

'That's damn-foolery. Vigilantes won't let you retire. Ain't a sheriff from here to the Mother Lode hears your name but what he gets goose-pimply and starts to looking around for rope. So if you got your eye on a Blackfoot squaw, make sure she's a fast traveler, because she'll need speed to keep up with you.'

He was telling the truth, of course. A reputation is sometimes easier to carve out than it is to run away from. John considered this as he watched Shep's face. Something was brewing there at Piegan City. That bunch of renegades outside would need no help in robbing any stagecoach or bank of the Territory, yet Shep evidently wanted him to join up.

'You must have something special,' he said.

'I have, and it's none of your ornery coach robbing, neither. None of your laying out in the rain with the ants and ticks crawling over you all night on some mountain grade waiting for a coach to come, and then probably more lead than gold for your trouble. Why, this is first class. 'Tain't robbery; it's an act o' war, with the best man in the Territory backing us up.'

'What do ye aim to do, go down to Virginny City and run out them Yankees that's took over the government and announce that the Territory jines up with the glorious states o' the Confederacy?'

'To hell with the Confederacy.' He saw the truculent sag of John's shoulders and hurried to add, 'And to hell with the Union, too, for that matter. I ain't interested in that ruckus they got back East. I wish every Yankee would kill a reb and git hung for it. All I care about is a little heavy color in my poke and maybe something in my gullet that won't freeze when the snow flies.' He sat down and talked seriously. 'John, this is the biggest cinch I run onto in all the years I been taking it down the long wahhoo. It's perfect, the pay's good, there's plenty excitement, and it's safe. Now there's a combine you ain't likely to find this side of Congress.'

'Last time I got talked into a sure thing there was a forty-man bushwhack laid at the other end of it.'

'Not this one there won't be. This time you'll be *backed* up by the vigilantes, you won't be against 'em.'

Rambo had fried the salt pork, and in the half inch of hot fat that remained in the pan he ladled sticky gobs of sourdough paste which quickly puffed to form doughgods. When it was done he dumped it all in a tin plate and carried it to John, who went to work with his bowie knife, eating in huge mouthfuls.

'What sort o' vigilante committee would have business with the likes o' you?' he asked.

'Captain's Brass's sort of vigilantes.'

John's eyes narrowed, and their gray was the color of bullet lead but he kept shoveling the salt pork and doughgods, washing them down with scalding tea.

He said, 'Seems to me like I heered about a man named Cap'n Brass being the bull moose up around American Flag.'

'He's the big hawg in them wallows, all right. Owns a stage line, a freight line, and he charges toll on twenty mile of mountain road, too, so he has all the other outfits coming to him with their hats in their hands. There's nothing small bore about the Cap'n.'

'What's he up to with you? Is he hiring men to rob his coaches so's he can cheat the St Louis insurance brokers?'

'No, but maybe it's a good idee. I'll mention it to him as soon as he comes.'

'Ye mean he's coming *here?*'

'I reckon, but you don't need to get spooky. If I say you're a friend of mine that'll be good enough for the Cap'n.'

John became more wary than ever. He slid his stool back a little so that someone coming unexpectedly through the door would not be directly behind him. He sat quiet and listened, having for a moment imagined that someone had called out in the distance, but there was nothing. Only the small movements of men on the porch outside. He saw Rambo get up and move around toward the shadowy end of the room and called out, 'Git back over thar so I can watch you.'

Shep said, 'How you talk! Rambo's your friend.'

'I stayed alive in this country since the year o' '49 by never trusting a friend half as far as an enemy.' He went on eating salt pork, but he no longer seemed very hungry. 'What sort

72

of a job has Cap'n Brass got laid out?'

'Why you care as long as it makes you money without risk?'

'I don't chase rabbits into blind holes. Now, maybe you didn't hear what I said. I asked what sort of job he had laid out.' John shifted the bowie from his right hand to his left. He slid to the edge of the stool and bent forward, a crouch with his right knee almost touching the floor, the butt of the Navy swinging out. It was all casual and it could have been accidental, but Shep went stiff and backed up.

'Hold on, now,' he said. 'Don't you go getting ringy, because you haven't a cause to. Here I am, offering you a chance to fill your jeans with some easy color and you–'

'What sort of a job's he got?'

'I was just saying. He's in the chips, see? The blue chips. So he aims to stay that way. Country's growing up, and the man owning the freight business will control 'er. Them's his words. Well, there's a mouse in the buttermilk – a young Yankee from Leavenworth way building a steamboat to run the upper Missouri between the Great Falls and American Flag.'

'What o' that?'

'Why, now we got the job of slowing the lad down so's maybe he'll listen to a good cash offer from the Cap'n when he comes around to buy.'

'A good cash offer like what?'

'How'd I know? Maybe like ten dollars.'

'What if he got stubborn and held out for a big figure like twelve dollars and fifty cents?'

'Why, that's where we come in. We bullet-blast him.'

'And you need my help to take care of one lone Yankee?'

'He's got a crew, forty, fifty men. It'd take some bullet lead.'

'And you could raid that camp at the Great Falls, right under the noses of that vigilance committee at Fort Benton, and still not get yourself whipsawed?'

'The Captain has a way of fixing things,' Shep said placidly. 'You don't need to worry, John. We'll shoot that outfit inside out and sell their pelts to the Blackfeet to make tobaccy pouches out of, and there'll be no trouble from Benton.'

'When you figure on doing the job?'

'Soon as Brass comes, maybe, or maybe not. That's up to him. Well, what do you say? Do you jine up?'

John wiped his bowie and put it away. 'Excuse me, but there's a strong smell o' rattlesnake in hyar.'

Rambo said, 'A man that draws back at the smell of rattlesnake should ought stay clear of a town like Piegan City.'

Shep said, 'That's right, John. This is no camp meeting we run out here. Anyhow, you done plenty worse things than raid a steamboat camp, so don't give me that sky-pilot dance. Tell you what, you jine up and I'll even name the brigade after you. Comanche John's Raiders, or something like. Think what a verse that'd make for the mule skinners to add to your song, you raiding a steamboat.'

John said, 'I been sitting hyar making up a plenty good verse to add on the song.' And he sang in a tuneless voice:

'Comanche John rode to Piegan town,
To Piegan town rode he,
To shoot holes through a renegade
A low-down son-of-a-bee.'

He slapped his homespuns and cried, 'Dang it all, that's prime good. I got a good notion to put a chunk o' bullet lead through your gizzard right now so's there'll be no chance of it going to waste.'

'Shoot me and you'd never get out of here alive.'

'Don't lay any short odds on whar I'll get out of alive.'

John had heard something. The ringing sound of a hoof on rock, the movement of men away from the cabin. Then the dog started to bark and he kept it up until somebody kicked him and he ran off with his *ki-yi!* fading in the night.

'Who's thar?' John asked.

His manner made Shep say, 'What's

wrong with you, anyhow? Never saw you so spooky. You come here with a posse on your trail? If you led a gang o'–'

'Put out the light.'

Shep did it, pinching the wick between his fingers and the heel of his hand. The fire was still burning in the stone fireplace but the tables and benches cast big shadows across the room, making it hard to see a man unless you knew his exact position. John had drawn his righthand Navy. He stood, looking careless, his jackboots spread, the barrels angled toward the ceiling, still listening. There were voices down by the corrals. One of them had a treble quality that carried well, and he recognized it. Captain Brass!

'Why, that's him now,' Shep said.

'Sure. It's the good Cap'n.'

'Thought you didn't know him.'

'I know him. I've known him in Californy and I've known him in I-dee-ho. The fact is, I rode down to American Flag chiefly to put a bullet through him, but the way things turned out I couldn't do it. But maybe tonight it'll be different.'

Shep moved and opened his mouth as though to shout a warning. He reconsidered, closed it, gulped.

'That's usin' your good judgment,' John said. 'Now you just stay whar ye be.'

Brass hadn't followed him. John was sure of that. He'd never have ridden up to Piegan

76

City openly if he'd known John was any-where around. But he knew now. Those fellows would tell him the moment he rode up, and he'd try to make certain that John never left the place alive.

Voices stopped. The night had suddenly become silent. Only the dog barking from a distance; the fire making little contraction sounds as it worked its way through the logs in the fireplace. A boot crunched on gravel.

John noticed that Rambo had disap-peared. 'Whar is he?' he asked. 'Rambo.'

'He ain't been here for five minutes.'

'Did he go out the back way?'

'I guess.' Shep, noticed that the gun was aimed at him, and took a step back. He was frightened, and in the long-slanting rays of the fire his face looked hollow and lumpy, his eyeballs protruding. 'Turn that thing the other way. If you think you can blast me and git out of here alive—'

'He went to tip off Brass that I was here.'

'If he did it wouldn't be my doing—'

'Stand whar ye be.' He took his time, tugged off a chaw of tobacco, spat at the fireplace, moved around the table with the gun at Shep's back. 'Now walk to the door. Slow. That's it. You open it when I tell ye to, but don't go outside. You just stand thar and yell, "Cap'n, he's got out the back way!" You remember that? And make sure you say it like you mean it or else I can't be answerable for anything this trigger finger o' mine happens to do.'

'I'm peaceful, John. You was always my friend. I wouldn't–'

'Open the door.'

Shep got hold of the latch. He took a deep breath and jerked the door open.

He was silhouetted with firelight behind him, and a man shouted, 'It's Shep! Hold your fire!'

The warning came too late. Someone pulled a trigger. The bullet struck Shep, in the muscle of his right shoulder and slammed him back against the door. He had presence of mind to roll aside, and he half fell, half dived to the ground.

He'd started to shout what John told him to. Now he was crawling away, mouthing every vile word in the Northwest.

John sprang over him. He pivoted and ran along the house, hidden by the shadow of the awning. When he neared the corner someone glimpsed him and shouted, 'There he is!' and cut loose with two Navy sixes.

He turned the corner amid flying lead. One of the bullets cut a splinter that stabbed itself through the flesh of his left arm with raw, paralysing pain.

Until that moment he hadn't fired. Powder flashes would merely have given away his position. A nest of men appeared directly ahead of him. He fired with both Navies and sent them scattering to cover.

Three steps and he was in the open, then he dived face foremost, rolled over once, and ended on hands and knees behind a rubbish heap.

There he could hear Brass shouting orders in his treble voice.

John whooped in answer, 'Maybe *you'd* like to take me, Brass. All even up, fair and square. One o' you and one o' me. Come along. I'll fight ye with my guns, or my bowie, or just with my hands. I'll even fight ye in the sluice pond, horse-and-alligator style.'

The shooting had tapered off, but at sound of his voice it came again, a sudden fusillade, the bullets tearing the dirt and ashes and glass of the rubbish heap and showering it over him.

He rolled over again, crawled for a distance, and came to one knee behind a stump. Men were circling toward a cluster of cabins and wickiups where they'd be able to pin him down. He fired into their midst and saw them scatter, every man for himself clawing for cover.

'Come on, ye he-wolves,' he whooped. 'Come and git it while it's hot. This is company night. I'm serving lead biscuits for supper, and all my beds are six feet deep.'

He kept retreating, close to the ground, found the cover of some buckbrush and afterward the entrance to a horse shed. The

shed was long and narrow, made of hori-
zontal poles. A deep cover of rotted hay and
manure had accumulated on the ground,
muffling his boots as he stood and walked.

He stopped a few strides short of the lower
door and listened for a moment. They were
still shooting, at what he didn't know, and
he could hear Brass, who had resorted to
curses and threats trying to get some sort of
order into the pursuit.

There was a pole corral beyond the shed.
Eight or ten horses, spooky from gunfire,
charged back and forth. He climbed the
fence and dropped inside. They were gone
at a gallop. He dodged among them,
reached the far fence, scaled it, splashed
across the creek that lay just beyond, walked
through jack timber to the pasture. The
gunpowder, cross-hobbled, had his head up
and ears cocked, watching him.

Chapter Five

A Widow Pitches Vittles

Comanche John walked toward the horse,
talking in an easy voice, and untied the
hobble string, first from the hind leg and
then from the fore. He had no bridle, so he

used the string to fashion a Blackfoot hacka-more, drew it tight, and mounted bareback.

'You had yourself a damn short rest, Gunpowder,' he said.

He'd got too much information for Brass's good, and he could trust him to run the legs off every horse in the camp trying to catch him before he could get a warning down to Pike Wilbur at his camp by the Great Falls.

The gunpowder ambled off at his usual wolf trot, hunting the shadow of evergreens. There was a trail, a poor one, winding among deadfalls and blocks of granite. Slowly the moon was coming up.

He reined around after a quarter mile of climbing and looked back. There was activity around the corrals. The gate bar was lowered, and two horsemen came in view. They wheeled around and waited. Five more men came out and they fanned across the clearing at a gallop.

John nudged his horse once again into movement. When the trail became steep he dismounted and walked ahead. In an hour he was at the high ridge, then, through the hours of morning, he descended successive slopes back toward the Missouri. It was late on the second day and far from the mountains when at last he sighted Pike Wilbur's boat camp.

He dismounted, aching and spavined from hours in the saddle, and sat cross-legged looking down at the camp. It was a couple of miles off, but all the heat distortion was gone from the air, and he could see with fine exactness, each detail minutely perfect.

A string of cabins had been built between a cottonwood grove and the river. The boat, much smaller than the steamboats one saw at Benton, was a frame with about half of its planking in place, standing on a cradle above the deep backwater of the river. A team of mules traveled in a weary circle, turning a whim that powered a circular saw. He could hear the drone of it intermittently, as well as shouting voices and the steady *ka-whack* of woodchoppers.

A bell rang shortly after sundown, and men strung back to the cabins. He estimated their number at about forty. A breeze sprang up with twilight, carrying the odor of wood smoke and cooking.

He hadn't eaten since the night before, and the sudden craving brought by the smell of food made him stand and grab for the pony's hackamore, but he reconsidered and didn't ride straight down. Brass, with his fresh horses, could have beaten him by many hours. He could have gone on to Benton and talked the vigilantes there into coming for him. Either way he'd have to be wary for a deadfall. It would be best to wait, to ride down after dark.

He gnawed off a cheekful of blackjack twist and satisfied himself with that.

With darkness, sounds of the camp died away, so he mounted and rode slowly down the cutbanks and across the flats. He caught glimpses of a fire through cottonwood timber, and it guided him. He drew up again at forty or fifty yards. There was no one in sight except a gangling, freckled-faced kid who had seated himself on a keg within the glow of the fire to pluck his five-string banjo. After some experimenting he located the melody of 'Old Rosin the Bow', and commenced singing in a sad and rather nasal voice:

'Hurrah for the choice of the nation!
Our chieftain so brave and so true;
We'll go for the great reformation,
    For Lincoln and Liberty, too.

Then up with our banner so glorious,
The star-spangled red, white, and blue,
We'll fight till our banner is victorious,
    For Lincoln and Liberty, too.'

Comanche John chawed and listened to him. He'd seen nothing to make him suspicious. Everything was peaceful, the men asleep. He clucked to the pony and jogged on into the firelight. He was sliding off, belly down and stirrupless, when the kid sensed him and sprang to his feet.

'Who in thunder be you?' he asked.

'Why, son, whar's your manners? Be ye a

Pike's Peaker or such type o' punkin roller that ye don't know that ain't a polite question in these parts? I've known men that'd shoot ye for asking no more, and that's a fact. O' course I come hyar as peaceful as a Chinee on St Patrick's day, with nothing but Christian brotherhood in my heart for everybody. Share and share alike, that's been my guiding motto.' He gestured at the banjo. 'Ye play well, son, but I didn't think much o' the sentiment in the song. Maybe you could favor me with one about the Hon'rable Jefferson Davis, President o' the Confederacy?'

'You mean the one about hanging him on a sour apple tree?'

'Dammit, no. I mean the one that goes:

'At the helm, Jeff Davis,
With your cohorts ridin' hard!
To the fore, Jeff Davis,
Win the day with Beauregard!'

The kid said, 'That's a new one on me, mister.'

'New one on ye! What's the trouble with young'ns these days? Don't they teach 'em the difference between right and wrong? Could be that you know the song about the famous road agent, Comanche John. That's a purty tune.'

'Everybody knows that,' the kid said, and

sang a couple of stanzas with measured sadness.

'John met a man named Bill McGurk,
    A gunman from Mo-hee,
They stopped the coach at Rocky Bar
    To commit a rob-er-ee;
They took the gold and silver,
    They took the greenbacks, too,
Oh! listen to the song I sing,
    I'll tell ye what they do:

'They ride to Orofino
    On the old Snake River trail,
They rob the coach at Pistol Rock
    And stop the Western mail,
But they captured Bill in Lewiston,
    They tossed him into jail
And they hung him to a cottonwood
    Ere John could go his bail.'

John sniffed once, saddened by the song and his memory of Bill McGurk. He'd been a great one with a Navy gun, Billy had, but he had a hankering for trade likker, and any road agent with such is putting himself up against the long percentages. He thought of others in the old crowd, of Boone Robel and Clubfoot George and The Deacon – every one of them a ring-tail ripper, and every one of them six feet underground. It was a risky business. A year or three down the long

85

coulee and a man's likely to get cut short or maybe a damned sight shorter. Sometimes it is a camp like Lewiston, busting at the seams with brand-new law and order; sometimes it's a stagecoach with a sleeper guard inside; and sometimes just a camp like this one, apparently as safe as grandma's parlor until the deadfall met a man with a yellow blaze of gunfire.

The kid was finished. He was holding the banjo under one arm, staring off into the darkness back of Comanche John. He noticed John watching him, and his eyes shifted back.

'What is it?' John asked.

'Nothing!'

He said it too quickly, too defensively. Comanche John was slouched as always. He swung around, thumb hooked in the band of his homespuns, but a saw-edge voice cut the night.

'Keep your hands clear, stranger.'

'Clear they be. I got the most innocent pair of hands between hyar and the state of Ioway.'

'All right, you keep 'em that-a-way because I wouldn't want to blast you apart with this old Jaeger gun. I had a hard day, and buryin' a man is too much trouble.'

'Why, no. I wouldn't want to put you to that sort of trouble, neither.'

'Who's with you?'

'*With* me? I ain't seen a soul. Nobody except this lad, here, and I reckon ye know him already.'

The man grunted something and came forward. He was huge and stoop-shouldered, forty or so, his face covered by tangled, reddish beard. Under one arm, cocked and pointed, was an old-time Jaeger rifle.

'What you want, snoopin' around here?'

'You're askin' what do I want? Right now I'd be satisfied if ye turned that rifle bar'l in some other direction.'

'She's pointed all right to suit me. I asked what you wanted in this camp.'

'I'm looking for a friend o' mine. Pike Wilbur.'

'He ain't here.'

Comanche John looked at his face closely, wondering whether he was telling the truth or not.

'I rode a considerable piece on a tired horse to see him, and if he's—'

'I said he ain't here.'

'Whar is he?'

He looked stubborn and suspicious for a few seconds before answering, 'I dunno.'

'When'll he be back?'

'Seems to me you're full up of questions. I don't know where Wilbur went, and I don't know if he'll ever git back.'

'Then I'll spread my robes and wait.'

'Oh, *will* you? Well, maybe we ain't hankering for your company.'

'White men in this country generally–'

'Don't tell me what we ought to do. This ain't Noo Yawk or Hannibal or any o' them big towns where all you do is whoop loud when you want a sheriff. This cursed country is crawling with road agents, and with Injuns and renegades, too. There's plenty of flat ground down the river if you're looking for a place to lay your robes. Now, I've talked, all I intend. You git on that horse and dust the bushes while you're still in one piece without any leaks.'

'Maybe this ain't Wilbur's boat camp at all. Maybe this is Brass's camp.'

'Ain't Brass's. If you're looking for Brass, he's downriver three or four mile nearer the falls.'

The man's massive hands kept opening and closing, and each time his forefinger seemed to bend harder around the trigger. John kept backing, wary of him, but not wanting to go.

'Pike be back tomorrow, maybe?'

The freckled kid spoke unexpectedly. 'Tonight, he said. He went to Benton. Him and the gal that inherited Faro Hill's share, and–'

The big man spun and took three long strides with the gun held out at arm's length, 'Rip, I got me a notion to bend this bar'l around your skinny neck.'

A woman shouted from off in the dark, 'No

you won't!' and the big man stopped. She charged into sight with an eight-gauge double gun tossed shoulder-high. She was in her early forties, gaunt and rangy, and strong as a man. She said, 'Wilcoxson, I told ye twenty times if I told ye once to quit picking on that poor, motherless child, and if ye threaten him again you'll be picking birdshot out o' your beam till next Christmas.'

'Damn it, Mrs Coppens–'

'And you watch your language in front of a woman. I took all I intend from the likes of you. Drop that rifle.'

'I'm on sentry duty here, and this black-whiskered stranger–'

'Drop it!'

He let the rifle fall, and the woman grunted her satisfaction. Then for the first time she took a good look at John. 'And who in the name o' Judas be you?'

'Name's Jones, and I'm nigh starved.'

The woman lowered her double gun and said, 'Now there's a houn' dog answer if I ever gave ear to one. He's hungry, he says. Hungry at this time o' night after me slaving over a hot kettle since before sunup this morning.' She wheeled around and bellowed toward a log house more substantial than the others and evidently the cook shanty.

'Wong, ye heathen, get up and kindle the fire. We got a pilgrim with his ribs showing.'

A middle-aged Chinese in loose shirt and

trousers appeared in the door holding a candle in one hand and a butcher knife in the other.

'You likee stew het up?'

'Heat it up. All of it. This one looks like he could eat like my poor dead husband's no-account relations.'

John untied the halter string and refixed it as a hobble. By the time he returned, a big iron kettle of buffalo stew and dumplings was thumping to a boil in the fireplace.

The smell of it made John so hungry he could scarcely walk, but he managed to reach the cookhouse door and sat cross-legged on the ground just beyond any direct light.

'Praise be your name, Mrs Coppens, you've revived my hope in the salvation o' the human race. I'd got to thinking the world was jug full of varmints without the charity to take a weary pilgrim off the rocky trail of life. "For I am a stranger with ye, and sojourner," and that's right out of the Psalms o' David, it is for a fact.'

'Bless me, you don't like a religious man with them Navies on your hips, but you do have the sound of one.'

'Don't let that gunmetal fool ye, ma'am. I just wear 'em so I'll have the right ballast on my horse. Share and share alike, that's my motto, and a Christian one, too.'

'Amen!' Mrs Coppens heaped stew on a sheet-metal plate, dripping deep to find the

90

tenderest morsels of buffalo hump. 'It's good to associate with a religious gentleman after all the low-down, unwashed, flea-bit varmints they got together in this camp. But *this* Sunday they ain't going to sit around and play cards. *This* Sunday every mother's son of 'em will be at church service or I'll blast 'em in the hocks with birdshot.' She explained, 'We got a preacher come to stay here for a spell.'

'It couldn't be my dear friend, the Reverend Parker, who just lately built a mission in that sump hole of wickedness and Yankee sympathy, American Flag.'

'That's him. You say you know him?'

'Ma'am, it was that same Reverend Parker that plucked me off the back trails of sin and set me forward along the ridgetops of righteousness.'

Mrs Coppens heaped buffalo and dumplings to the limits of the plate and handed it to him. John thanked her and commenced spearing chunks with his bowie and carrying them to his mouth. He'd forgotten how good things could taste. He was half starved, but that wasn't the only thing. This wasn't squaw cooking or prospector slum. This was white-woman cooking, and the likes of it he hadn't tasted since he'd drifted north from the Oregon Trail. After stowing away the plateful and waiting for another, he looked up and saw Wilcoxson glowering at him from the shadows, twenty feet away.

'Sight o' you don't help my dee-gestion any,' John muttered. Then to Mrs Coppens, 'What's got this camp so ringy?'

'Road agents. Country's full of 'em ever since the vigilantes got their hangropes busy down at Virginny City.'

Wilcoxson said, 'I'll tell you what's got us ringy. We heard Comanche John was headed this way from American Flag.'

'You mean Comanche John, the one they sing the song about?'

Mrs Coppens said, 'That's him. Another one o' the ten thousand road agents they run out of Californy.'

'"Judge not so ye be not judged;" that's what the Parson always said. Seems to me I heered this Comanche John had his good points together with his bad.'

'Maybe, but if that black sinner rides in hyar I'll pour rat pizen in his dumplings.'

John tasted his new plateful for flavor.

Wilcoxson said, 'How come you hold Comanche John in such favor, Jones? Could be he's a friend of yours?'

'Never met him, face to face that is.'

'Saw a print-shop dodger of him in Benton. Five hundred in gold ree-ward. Sheriff of Beaverhead County offered it. Dodger had a picture of Comanche John. Black-whiskered old wolf, gray eyes, five feet eight, broad in the beam, and long-armed. You ain't run into anybody answering that description, have you?'

John met his gaze. 'Have you?'

'Ain't noticed.'

Mrs Coppens said, 'Why, Jones, you answer the thing yourself. Just shows you can't tell the difference between saint and sinner by the size of his boots.'

John mopped up the last drops of gravy and sat back with hands crossed over his stomach. He seemed sleepy and off guard, but his eyes remained quick beneath the droopy lids, and he watched the camp for signs of trouble.

He hadn't known about the five hundred in gold that the sheriff of Beaverhead County was offering for him. Five hundred was considerable, for one of these Pike's Peak emigrants, anyhow. Upward of a dozen of them had crawled from the wickiup to look at him, but they were all out of sight again.

Mrs Coppens blew out the candle and came outside. 'Pilgrim, if there's anything you need, just help yourself. I'm going to hit the shucks.'

He said good night to her. The redheaded kid had all the while been twanging the strings of his banjo. He stopped and was looking off through the dark. He had a sharp sense of hearing, and for the second time in half an hour it gave John his warning.

He moved back to deeper shadow. In half

a minute there was a snap of dry bushes, the clatter of a hoof on stone. Then eight men rode into view, single file.

By that time John was around the house. He was looking for Wilcoxson, saw him, walked close.

'Could be they're looking for Comanche John,' he said.

Wilcoxson spun around and found himself facing the muzzle of an unholstered Navy.

'What the devil—'

'I ain't been here tonight. Nobody has. Understand?'

'Yeah!' whispered Wilcoxson. And he repeated, 'Yeah.'

The first of the men, short and powerful, swung down and walked on stiff, spavined legs, a sawed-off shotgun across his arm. The others ranged themselves along the shadowy edge of the clearing, suspicious and watchful.

'You, kid!' the short man said to Rip.

'Me?'

'O' course *you*. Damn it, step lively!'

Rip was scared. He moved a few halting steps.

John said, 'Wilcoxson, you better get thar and head the lad off before he says something he shouldn't ought.'

Wilcoxson took a step, but Mrs Coppens strode into view. She shouted, 'Hold on, stranger, you don't need to come in this camp and talk to a child that way. I ain't going to stand for it. What's your aim, any-how, riding in here at an hour when all decent folk are asleep?'

The man laughed and said, '*You* aren't asleep.'

'Who be ye?'

'I'm Jack Hartley, Fort Benton.'

'A vigilante!'

'What's wrong with being a vigilante?'

'Nothing's wrong with 'em till they get to thinking they're greater than the Almighty, and after that they get to be as bad or worse than the ones they hang. What are you look-ing for?'

'Wolves.'

'Plenty wolves howling out in the breaks.'

'We're after the two-legged kind.'

'Why, it might be we got some of them around, too. And again we might not. You looking for any particular wolf?'

'A black-whiskered one, unless he's shaved. One by the handle of Comanche John.'

Mrs Coppens turned slowly, and her eyes traveled to the door of the cookhouse where Comanche John had been sitting, but now he was gone. Her jaw was set hard and her lips pursed. She kept rubbing her big, man-nish hands on her dress. Finally she grunted and said, 'Way I hear it, everybody betwixt Sacramento and British America is looking for that one. Anyhow, I still don't under-stand why you'd look for him here.'

'We got it on pretty good authority it was this camp he was headed for.'

'Well, I ain't seen anybody calling himself Comanche John.'

'No strangers at all come here today?'

Rip was about to say something, but Mrs Coppens cut him off. 'You git to bed. How many times—'

'Hold on. You, kid – what were you going to say?'

'Nothing!'

'You seen no strangers?'

'Nobody but—' He stopped, fearing both Mrs Coppens and the vigilante. 'Nobody but Jones.'

'Who's he?'

Mrs Coppens said, 'Preacher. Man of the cloth, practically. You haven't taken to hanging 'em for that reason, have you?'

'Not unless they need it.' Hartley laughed. He was tired and short-tempered, but it was plain that Mrs Coppens had won his admiration. He gave up trying to learn anything from her and turned towards his men. 'Qualey and Janes, you circle the bushes and see if you can spot that gunpowder horse.' Then back to Mrs Coppens, 'How about a drink of water?'

'Whole river of it yonder.'

'I'd rather have this.' He walked to the bucket she'd just carried up from the spring. She watched with silent hostility as he lifted it and drank from its lip. Other men rode up, and it was passed from hand to hand. Hartley said in a voice intended to be conciliatory, 'We shook plenty of the bushes since we got wind of the Comanche this morning. Turned his trail at a meat hunter's shanty down on the Muddy about noon. Lost it again, but he was headed this way. There's five hundred in gold waiting in Bannack City for the one that gets him.'

'Five hundred for *you*.'

'Our vigilance committee accepts no rewards. All we want is Comanche John.'

'If you catch him, what then?'

'We'll hang him, of course.'

'Yonder in Missouri where I hail from they always give a man a trial before hangin' him.'

'This isn't Missouri.' He turned then and glimpsed Wilcoxson, who all the time had stood near the corner of the house, stiff and scarcely breathing. 'Who are you?'

Wilcoxson moved suddenly. 'Me? I'm Wilcoxson. I'm lookout.'

'Then you'd see anybody that came into camp?'

'Yeah.'

'Any strangers about?'

He signed in the negative, weaving his head from side to side. Qualey and Janes rode back and Hartley asked if they'd seen anything. Qualey, a tall, big-boned man, said, 'No.'

'You didn't take very long.'

'Damn it, you try to pick a gunpowder roan out of that herd. It's as black as a gambler's heart out there.'

They were all evil-tempered after a solid eighteen hours in the saddle, and yet a fifty-mile ride from home.

Hartley, still hesitating, sniffed the air and said, 'Vigilantes get hungry, too. Is that stew I smell?'

Mrs Coppens said, 'Only thing I smell around here is skunk.'

'All right, ma'am. We'll get out.' He mounted, bending his tired legs with obvious effort. 'You're making a mistake, though. The only reason we hang these wolves is to protect you.'

He rode off then, leading his men down-river.

They were out of sight but still Mrs Coppens and Wilcoxson watched, tense and silent. Then there was movement behind them, and Comanche John slouched into view. He was holding his right-hand Navy. Not pointing it – apparently he was just appraising its weight. He said something and dropped it back in the holster.

'You a Christian!' Mrs Coppens brayed. 'I ought to get my scatter-gun–'

'No ye shouldn't, because I told ye I was regenerated with the power of the Word, and so I be. I'm one o' the Parson's prize converts, and in that he'll back me up as soon as he gets back from Benton.'

'You're Comanche John, that's who you be, a no-good, shiftless, gun-shootin', coach-robbin' varmint that was born to die with his toes three feet off the ground.'

'I'll die between clean white sheets with my boots all polished standing by the wall. So a gypsy gal told me one day in Denver City.'

'Anyhow, we saved your hide. Me and Wilcoxson. And now that we've done it, you better catch that salt-and-pepper horse of yours and drift, because we got a few ornery boys yonder in the shanties, and they might get some hanging ideas of their own.'

'Not when they find out why I came here.'

'Well, why did you?'

'Because I had an idee o' saving your hides.' He could see that she didn't believe him. 'I came to tell you about what Cap'n Brass is fixing up for ye. He's got half the renegades in the territory shacked up at Piegan City ready to cut loose on this camp whenever he gives the word.'

She grunted and said, 'No use trying to git yourself a welcome that way. My advice to you is saddle and ride while you're still able.'

'Ye don't believe me?'

'I don't believe, and I don't disbelieve. I'll wait and see. But you don't need to think them Pike's Peakers yonder in the shack will believe. Not by a jugful. So stay if ye like, but do it at your own risk.'

Chapter Six

Spy Trouble

John had a bath in the river and fought off mosquitoes while waiting for the night breeze to dry him. The camp looked deserted when he got back, but he could hear them talking inside the bunkhouse. Mrs Coppens had told the truth. Those Pike's Peakers were getting ornery.

John cursed them suitably, yawned, and went to sleep on a heap of shavings where axmen had been trimming down some cottonwood beams. Late in the night he sat up with the awareness that riders were coming from downriver.

He recognized the Parson's voice, and Dallas Hill's. He wondered if she planned to stay there at the camp to look after her interests. He wished she wouldn't. It would be a bad ruckus for a girl. Then he recalled how she'd handled that side-hammer pistol and decided maybe such a ruckus might be her style. He waited until the jingle of spurs and bridle links showed them to be close and said, 'Hey, yonder!'

It was Pike Wilbur who answered, 'Who

is it?'

The Parson said, 'Why, it's that varmint, Comanche John, come here after us telling him to stay away.'

John said, 'For twenty-five year, Parson, I been in the habit o' going whar I danged well please no matter what I was told.'

They came up, and the Parson saw him. 'Thar ye be! Why'd ye quit Robbers' Roost?'

'Robbers' Roost ain't all she used to be.'

'You mean there's honest folk live there these days?'

'No, I don't. I mean that camp's taken a turn for the worse. Cap'n Brass is bossing her these days. Seems like he's calling the tune nigh every place.'

'He ain't here!'

'Yet.'

'What do you mean by that?'

'I mean he's got a private army o' renegades yonder at Piegan just spilin' to burn gunpowder, and I don't imagine it'll be on any crusade to purify the territory.'

Pike said, 'You think he's getting ready to raid our camp?'

'Yep, that's his idee. Asked me to jine up. Shep did. That's Shep Shepherd, a bushwhack specialist from down in I-dee-ho. Couldn't get all his plan. Brass showed up at just the wrong time.'

He went on then and recounted his experiences since leaving American Flag.

Pike Wilbur said, 'You don't think he'll try anything tonight?'

'Nobody can figure what a man like Brass'll do. He guessed I'm on my way here or he wouldn't have tipped off the Benton vigilantes.'

'How long since they left – the vigilantes?'

'Maybe – two hours.' He squinted at the moon. 'Or closer on to three.'

'No. He wouldn't risk it with them ranging the country. He'll wait.' He jerked his head down at the shanties. 'They roused the crew, I suppose.'

'Why yes, they raised a little commotion, and I suppose I'd of been handed over, only I had a gun on Wilcoxson.'

'They know who you are, then?'

'I'd imagine.'

The Parson said, 'O' course they know. John, ye gone and messed things up for fair, leading the vigilantes *here*. I told ye in American Flag that Pike couldn't afford to get tied up with your kind.'

John doffed his hat and held it over his heart, saying, 'May I ask your pardon, Reverend, for saving your hide?'

Dallas said sharply, 'What else could he do but come? It was either that or let us get caught in Brass's deadfall. If those Benton vigilantes want to side with him, why we'll have to fight them, too.'

John chuckled and spat. 'Now there's a

fight I'd like. All the stranglers on one side.'

Pike Wilbur said, 'Sure, Dallas. He had to come. For *our good* he had to come, though still it's a tough piece of luck. I need their confidence in at Benton.'

John said, 'If you'd like me to shuck out–'

'No. I want you to stay. I'll make it worth your while. I'll even cut you in on the profits, if there are any.' He glanced at Dallas and added, 'With the consent of my partner, that is.'

'I ain't particularly interested in the profit,' John said. 'I used to be in a business whar I traded lead for gold and the profit was nigh onto a thousand percent, and the Parson talked me into quitting it. I do git a little rusty for excitement now and again, though.'

The men inside one of the shacks had heard them and were appearing one after another in the door.

'There's trouble for me,' Wilbur said.

John spat. 'Them Pike's Peakers?'

'They're building the boat, and not being paid too often, either. I can't afford to have them rear back at me.'

He walked across, and Wilcoxson, huge as a grizzly on his hind legs, plodded a few steps to meet him.

'Know who he is?' Wilcoxson asked, gesturing past him at Comanche John.

'Yes.'

'Mean you know he's Comanche John and

still let him stay in the camp?'

'I'll decide who can stay in this camp, and I'll decide it without asking your advice.'

Wilcoxson bellowed, 'Dammit, we don't go along with that. We don't mind work and slow pay and poor grub, but we ain't having truck with any road agents.'

He'd said 'we', including the men grouped behind him. Wilbur looked at them. The vigilantes had frightened them, and now they were rebellious.

They were members of the emigrant class lumped off as 'Pike's Peakers' – antislavery settlers in Kansas who'd been burned out by Quantrell's bushrangers, and had struck out for the gold camps in the Pike's Peak region near Denver City. It had been a tough trip through heat and dust and dried-up streams with bone-bag stock and crippled wagons, and they dragged the last miles down from Fort Laramie to find Denver City over-crowded with a thousand other flat-broke emigrants that had preceded them. But reports were coming down from the north telling of a river called the Snake where the gold diggings were practically limitless, and a man with a pan and shovel could wash out his stake in a single season, or with hard luck maybe two. So they got together a few supplies and joined the great surge north-westward, over mountains, and then over the dry-bone hills where a man could see his oxen die of thirst while looking down on the Snake surging through its gorge below. Reports of the Snake River diggings had been exaggerated. It was poor scratch, mostly, with the rich gulches and bars long before taken over by the Californy men. There was good money being paid for freighters and artisans, and some of them left the train, but most of them stuck together, going to Idaho City, to Orofino. Then with news of even greater strikes in a wilderness called Montana they turned eastward. Their stock was crippled and dying, their wagons rawhided together, but somehow they dragged across the terrible Lolo to Hellgate and fabulous Virginia City where again they were too late. Abandoning the hope of easy riches, they looked for farming land and found a strip of river bottom that suited them near the Deer Lodge. It was rich and well watered, better than anything they'd known in Kansas, but they were without stock or supplies, so their womenfolk stayed behind to set up homes while the men went north to Last Chance, and eventually found a place where they could all be together in Wilbur's boat crew.

Wilbur looked around at them now. They were rough and dirty, brutalized by their endless struggle against poverty and the frontier.

'We want our pay,' Wilcoxson said.

'You'll get your pay when it's due you.

You'll keep getting half as you go along and the other half when the job's done, just like we agreed.'

Wilcoxson's voice was raw and aggressive. 'It's owin' to us, and by grab we want it.'

Wilbur laughed. He did it easily, without offense, trying to quiet their antagonism. 'Listen, boys. You sleep on this. It'll look different to you by daylight.'

A gangling, hook-nosed man shouted, 'There was vigilantes rode down and through this camp. Californy men and killers, too, or I don't know the sign. What if they found out we was hidin' a road agent? Nothing a Californy man would rather do than swing a Pike's Peaker.'

Wilbur raised his voice. 'They'll hang nobody in this camp! If anybody gets hanged in this camp, *I'll* do it.'

It wasn't a threat, but it made them stop and look at him. The hook-nosed man grumbled, 'Anyhow, we ain't getting shacked up with any bad man like–' He checked himself and peered beyond Wilbur at Comanche John, who'd stopped at a distance of twenty-five or thirty steps and was slouched against a stack of squared cottonwood timbers. 'Like Comanche John,' he muttered.

Wilbur said, 'You don't want to believe all the verses of that song they sing. If it hadn't been for Comanche John I wouldn't be here to pay you a single cent. I'd be dead in

American Flag. Maybe he's even saved your lives by coming here.'

Wilbur had them listening then, so he went on and told about the near hanging in American Flag, and about the news that John had carried from Piegan City.

None of them spoke after he'd finished. They waited for Wilcoxson. He'd been elected wagon captain back on the Little Blue thirteen months before, and to most of them he was still the leader, though they wouldn't follow him into anything without a vote.

Wilcoxson kept opening and closing his hands, looking down at their shoe-leather palms while deciding what to say. He wanted to leave and take the men with him, that was plain enough, but they wouldn't have gone with half their money owing them, and rather than take a stand and be defeated in the vote he said, 'All right. We'll sleep on it. But I ain't having any business with road agents.'

The entire camp was roused now, among them a dozen Californy men – scouts, meat hunters, the boat foreman. One, big and red-whiskered, called Jim Swing, shot a stream of tobacco juice and hitched up his pants, saying, 'What's wrong with you Kansas punkin rollers? I count up twenty-eight of ye. Could it be that one man has the whole pack of ye scairt out?'

107

'We're not scared. We're not scared of you, Swing, nor of all your Californy bunch put together. And we ain't scared of him. It's just that we're honest and hard-working, and we don't–'

'This ain't Missouri. This ain't even the trail to Oregon. This is Montana Territory. This is the wild Nor'West. She's tougher'n hell and twice as wide. Maybe ye do have to shack up with a road agent. By grab, I didn't bring my pedigree along with me. Maybe I didn't even bring my right name. A name's a damn unimportant thing and likely to get mislaid along the way. I'll wager half the men north o' Fort Hall left the States two jumps ahead of the sheriff and one ahead of the Union draft. Past history be hanged; I'd rather have the Comanche's guns on my side than agin' me.'

Wilcoxson was like an ill-tempered grizzly, but he didn't argue; and John slouched forward and said, 'Why, gents, this is the best welcome I've had since the town o' Yallerjack. Didn't hear the word "rope" said once. So if ye like, I'll pitch my robes. And by the way, nobody except you boys knows for sure I'm hyar, so we might as well keep it that-a-way. You just forget all about me being Comanche John. From here on the name is Jones. *Jones*. That's spelled the same way as Smith, only backward.'

Extra sentries were put out for the

remainder of the night, but there was no alarm. In the morning John saddled one of the company horses and followed the buffs downriver until he caught sight of Brass's steamboat camp. There he dismounted and picketed his horse.

The sun was hot with midmorning, but it produced no heat wave, no mirage. He could see the half-finished cabins and corrals with fine exactness. A crew with horses and skid boats worked cottonwood timber a quarter mile upstream. Sun River flowed in, slow and yellowish, from the west. Downstream he could see a hint of mist rising from the Black Eagle Falls, and the dark gash of the canyon below it swinging from east to northeast toward Fort Benton.

He sat through the heat of midday; dozed through afternoon. At sundown he got up and stretched himself. He still had an hour to wait; then, with the first stars appearing, he rode downhill, keeping to brushy coulees until he was half a mile from the camp. He tied his horse in a patch of willow brush and went on afoot.

Sounds carried well with the heavy heat of day gone from the air, and he could hear voices, the laughter of men, He stopped where a fence of green aspen poles had been newly built around a pasture. Fourteen or fifteen head of work stock grazed inside, there were some ragged box-elder trees beyond, and through them he could see the gables and chimneys of two cabins and the occasional flicker of an open fire.

He waited another ten minutes as twilight thickened, then he swung over the fence and walked straight across the pasture. A breed kid was working on a bay saddle horse with a currycomb, getting cockleburs out of his mane. He saw John without stopping.

'Good evenin',' John said, and took time to run a hand over the horse's sleek rump. 'Cap's horse?'

'I theenk, sure,' the kid answered in his pleasant French Cree accent.

'Cap'n around?'

'I theenk – over at the beeg cabin.'

'Shep there, too?'

'Shep?' He stopped combing.

'Yes, Shep. Tall, dirty renegade from Piegan City. I wouldn't be surprised if he had his right wing in splints.'

'Oh, heem!' The kid made a bad face. 'Sure, he's there. Heem and plenty more.'

John went on, and while climbing a high pole gate had another quick view of the camp. They'd set up a whim saw and carpentry sheds at this right, and what looked like the keel of the boat was being put together on a scaffold that overhung the river. The cabins, half of them still without roofs, were a hundred yards upstream. Farther inland was a house of heavy logs, obviously the camp headquarters. A light burned inside it, but most of the men seemed to be gathered around a fire that had been built where the bank slanted down toward the river.

Someone was coming. Only a Chinese carrying two buckets of water on a yoke across his shoulders. John walked past him and stopped in the shadow of the carpenter sheds. He listened for running feet, first sign that someone had recognized him, but the camp was perfectly calm. He kept going, but not in the open now. Not with Shep and that Piegan bunch around to recognize him. He worked his way through willows and boxelders until a scant twenty steps separated him from the fire. A good many men were sprawled around with their boots thrust toward it, chewing tobacco, talking, spitting at the flames.

John bit off a freshener for his own chaw and settled down to listen.

What he heard was the usual coarse talk, the bawdy stories, and profanity, with now and then a stray mention of himself, Pike Wilbur, or Dallas Hill. Someone had left the big house and was coming that way. Only the shadow of him was visible, but John knew it was Shep Shepherd.

They quieted down a trifle when they saw him, a tall scarecrow of a man, face lopsided from tobacco, his right arm wrapped in a filthy bandage.

111

Shep had overheard some remark about Dallas Hill and said, 'You keep your lip from flappin' about that gal, Dillman. When we bust that Pike's Peaker camp she belongs to me.'

'Like hell,' a big, rough man said. 'If we get hold of *that* filly, she'll belong to Brass.'

They all laughed, Shep along with them, and somebody said, 'Shep, you'll get – the old gal – that widder named Mrs Coppens. I heered plenty about her. Curtis stopped there for victuals a while back and said she was rougher'n the road to Laramie.'

'She'll be gentled down some when I get through with her. I got a way with women. Keep 'em locked up, beat up, and bare-footed, that's my style.'

'That ought to be worth while to see; when we going to get the chance.'

'We'll git it. We'll bust that camp wide open.'

'Wish it'd be quick,' Dillman said. 'Mighty dull time I had since I joined up with you. Ain't shot so much as a Chinee.'

Shep sneered, 'You shoot as good as you talk?'

'Damned right I do!'

'Well, don't get your sweat hot.'

A blond fellow, little more than a kid, said, 'I hope Comanche John's there. That's the notch I'd like to carve.'

Dillman said, 'Listen to the button! You'd

have to hawg-tie him to get him in rifle range of Comanche John.'

'Comanche John's a big bluff if you want my opinion, and I ain't too sure about you, Dillman. Nobody's calling me–'

'Shut up!' Shep said. 'I'll have no ruckus while the boss is here. They'll be plenty chance for you to show off your brand of shootin'. Might be even Comanche John himself'll be there to liven things up.'

'The Comanche ain't closer'n Idaho.'

'We'll find out.'

'How?'

'I said we'd find out, didn't I!'

John's eyes narrowed when he heard the tone in which Shep asked the question. He'd promised to find out, and he'd done it with a swagger of confidence, the way of a man who owns a secret. He had some source of information inside Wilbur's camp. It could have been Wilcoxson, or anybody.

Shep sat down, cross-legged, and loaded his pipe from the pouch of cut-plug tobacco at his belt. He lighted it with a brand from the fire and went on talking, telling in a loud, swaggering voice what they'd do to Wilbur's camp when the time was right.

'When'll it be right?' Dillman asked.

'Why, whenever the Cap'n says so. *He'll know;* don't you worry about the Cap'n.'

The men started to stretch and yawn, and one by one they got up and walked back in the direction of the cabins. Talk shifted to small things, and almost died altogether. Comanche John had been watching the big log house. A light had been burning there all night, and once in a while he'd noticed a man's shadow against one of the parchment windows. Then the light blinked out, and two men walked to the door.

The thought occurred to him that one of them might be the spy he was looking for.

He moved back, swiftly but with care, for there was little sound now except for the snapping of coals beneath the ash of the fire, and took long strides around the bank, the cabins, and reached the far side of the house.

The men had paused there and were talking. One of them was Captain Brass. He knew that by the treble carrying quality of his voice. The other's voice was deeper and unfamiliar.

They walked slowly into the moonlight, Brass tall and erect as usual, the other man about four inches shorter, his hat pulled far forward shading his face.

They seemed to be walking toward the corrals.

John circled and came up behind the corrals on the bluff side. They were more extensive than he expected – a maze of high pole fences zigzagging through brush and small clearings. He crossed one after another. It took three or four minutes. Brass said something, his voice coming from an unexpected direction. He'd gone too far. He started back, then stopped when a gate creaked open and hoofs thudded at a swift trot westward.

John followed, running, but he was afoot and quickly outdistanced. The man had a good mile start before John reached his horse and got into the open.

Chapter Seven

Deadly Crossfire

Comanche John rode to the rimrocks and stopped to breathe his horse. It was bright moonlight, and he had no trouble seeing the man across the level prairie country. He seemed to be headed west toward the Benton freight road.

John gave him a quarter-hour start and followed. After covering about five miles the man turned back, almost retracing his steps, and dropped from sight over the rim of a coulee. John didn't catch sight of him again, though he scouted the country until almost daylight.

He rode to camp, sleepy and hungry, and was challenged by Jim Swing.

'Oh, you!' Swing said, lowering his rifle when he saw who it was. 'You gave me a start for a second.'

'Somebody ride down hyar about two hours past midnight?'

'Not by me they didn't. My watch has been quiet as a Quaker meetin'.'

'Who else is on watch?'

'Gregg and Watson up here. Tobel and that nephew o' his over by the bluffs. And I guess the Pike's Peakers got the river watched. Anyhow, they're supposed to. But nobody came. You can hear the prairie dogs scratchin' down under the ground, it's the quiet, and I'd o' heard the sentry sing out.'

John looked around at the bluffs. No horseman could have approached on a bright moonlight night without being seen. He rode around, speaking to the other sentries, but they told the same story. Nothing had disturbed them since they came on watch at midnight.

He still couldn't get it out of his head that the man had ridden down there. He slept for a while and got up to the sound of Mrs Coppens's clanging on the suspended wagon tire that served as a grub bell.

She glared on seeing his sleepless eyes and said, 'By grab, you got a jug hid in the bush, or you tooken to night-ridin' after stage-coaches?'

'I been kept awake by varmints.' He put a

heap of sourdough flapjacks and crisp salt pork on his tin plate and asked, 'You ain't had an extra boarder this morning, have ye?'

'Nary a one. Just the usual pack o' wolves.' Then she thought of someone and said, 'Unless you have ref'rence to Blair. He's new back from Fort Benton.'

She'd indicated a man seated on the ground by the near corner of the bunkhouse. John looked at him, stopped, and looked at him again. He'd seen him before somewhere, and his name hadn't been Blair.

'When'd he get here?'

'I dunno. He wasn't for grub pile last night. Reckon he came in through the early watch.'

That meant before midnight, so if Mrs Coppens was right he'd already arrived before John left Brass's camp.

'Who said he came through the early watch?'

'River sentries. Overhead talk of it not ten minutes ago.'

John ate and looked at the man. They'd met, all right, but it was a considerable time ago. His mind kept retracing all the convolutions of his back trail, trying to fit the man in, but it wasn't easy. He'd met a heap of people in that gold-crazy country that stretched from Sacramento to Fraser River.

Blair seemed to be about average height, much as you could tell with him sitting down. He was clean-shaven, thirty or so. His skin, burned brown as a Cree moccasin, indicated he wasn't one of the thousands new come from the East to escape the Union draft.

'He work here?' John asked Mrs Coppens.

'Wilbur hired him to map the river. He ain't like you ignorant mining men. He understands figures and compass needles and slope boards and such.'

Blair finished his breakfast, put down his plate, and walked over, placing his feet down in the slightly toed-in manner of one who has worn moccasins instead of boots the greater share of his life.

'You're Comanche John,' he said.

'So I be.' And instantly, at sound of his voice, John knew where they'd met. Fort Walla Walla. He hadn't been Blair then. He'd gone by the name of Stephens. He'd been a clerk for the Hudson's Bay Company at the Belly River post and had done well for himself until the old factor, Dom MacKay, finally drank himself to death and his replacement from Winnipeg noticed the wide discrepancy between trade goods and the bale count of beaver pelts. Turned out by the Company, he'd operated as an independent, trading whiskey for furs on both sides of the border.

'You don't remember me?' Blair said.

'I do now. We met at the Drover's Bar in Walla Walla and played monte together.

That was three years ago. I recollect some other things, too. I recollect ye had trouble with the Injuns out at the rendezvous and killed a half-breed named Joe Plaune on account of his wife.'

'His *squaw*,' said Blair, smiling without denial.

'Squaw to you but his wife to him. Injuns and Chinee feel the same about their families as hum'n beings do, I reckon. They'd o' hung ye in Walla Walla if they'd got hold of ye that night.'

He said defensively, 'You killed a man in Walla Walla, too.'

'It war in Lewiston, he war looking for trouble, and I never shot him in the back.'

Blair's face looked thin and mean. His eyes shifted around the camp trying to see whether anyone had overheard. He said through his teeth, 'I never shot that breed in the back no matter what lies they spread about me in Walla Walla.'

'All right, so ye didn't. I wasn't thar in the tepee to see.'

Blair licked his lips and decided to smile. 'Anyhow, live and let live. You made your mistakes, too, and I'm not talking.'

John finished breakfast, got up, and walked to the river where he cleaned his plate, using mud to emulsify the grease and a handful of sand from a bar to burnish the sheet metal. When he started back, Blair was waiting for him.

'I was at Benton. Those vigilantes there have a pretty good idea where to find you.'

'What you mean – that I ought to shake the bushes?'

'You suit yourself about that. It's your neck.'

'Benton, hey? Rode down last night.'

Blair met his eyes. 'Yes. I got here just after dark. Why?'

'You're might sharp on that point,' John drawled and walked back to drop his plate in the plunder box.

Through the day he was indolent, lying in the shade, chewing tobacco. Apparently he had no interest in Blair, but something in his manner caused Dallas to say, 'You don't trust him, do you?'

'Only two men in the world I put trust in – the Parson and Sam Colt.'

Blair didn't leave camp. He bedded down in the shack used by the Californy men and was still there when John got up in the morning. John was still suspicious of him, and more so than ever when he talked with the Pike's Peakers and found that Wilcoxson was the only sentry who would vouch for the time of his arrival two nights before.

That night John awoke and knew instantly that something was wrong.

He sat up and listened. It was dark, with a thin veil of clouds blown across the moon.

Wind was creaking the cottonwoods. He pulled on pants and boots, strapped the Navies around him. Through an opening in the trees he had a view of the camp, but there was no movement. Something, however, had awakened him. A sound, or just his instinct. A man gets a feel for danger and alarm after enough years of dodging it down the long coulee.

He walked to the open door of the Californy shanty. Men were snoring inside. He decided not to awaken them. He'd just tugged off a chaw of tobacco when he heard horses galloping in the pasture. They were alarmed and skittish. The wind could have frightened them, or it could have been someone roping a mount.

He could see no one in the pasture when he got there. It took five minutes to locate the gunpowder and get close enough to mount, then he rode bareback through the gate leading down to the river bank.

A man loomed unexpectedly. It was Wilcoxson, on sentry duty.

'Who goes thar?' Wilcoxson shouted, drawing back.

'Why, hello, Zeph,' John drawled, calling him by his first name. 'I see you're awake for a change.'

'Never saw me asleep on sentry duty.' The big man plodded up in his bowed, long-armed manner, his Jaeger rifle angled up from near the ground.

'Mind pointing that some other way?'

Wilcoxson shifted the barrel a couple of degrees. 'Where you headed this time of night?'

'Why, I like to ride when it's quiet, giving thought to this and that. Ain't anybody else with the same idee, Zeph? Somebody just now leaving camp, for instance?'

'No!' He said it too forcefully.

'You ain't great shakes as a liar.'

'No man's going to call me a liar even if he does pack twenty notches in his gun.'

'Zeph, it's to a man's credit, being a poor liar. Shows he ain't had much experience. Who was it just rode out of the pasture? Was it Blair?'

'I said–'

'I heered what ye said!' His voice became harsh and he nudged the gunpowder a trifle forward, bending to watch Wilcoxson's eyes. 'He caught a horse and left by this gate, otherwise he'd likely stir up a sentry he couldn't trust.'

'I told you–'

'War he headed to Brass's camp?'

Wilcoxson, caught in the lie, turned stubborn and savage. His big hands were locked around the rifle as though he intended to bend it double.

John said, 'Dammit, answer me.'

'I don't know, and it's none o' your business if I did.'

'He went downriver.'

'You ain't trailin' him out o' here! You got a grudge against Blair and aim on bushwhack. That's what—'

'Get out o' my way.'

'You ain't leaving camp!' Wilcoxson swung the rifle around, but John's horse was too close and the barrel struck its neck. Wilcoxson took a step back, trying to get free; then he saw John's shoulder move, a mere hitch, apparently, but one of the Navies was clear of its holster and pointed down on him across the horse's mane.

'Hand me that rifle, butt first,' John said.

He rode with it to the marge of the river, bent over, and rammed it, muzzle down, deep in the muck.

'Thar she is, Zeph. Now go ahead and take your pot shot.'

Zeph recovered the gun, but he knew better than try to shoot it. With its barrel full of mud it would backfire and blow his head off. He stood wiping it under the sleeve of his shirt as John rode downriver.

John was half a mile from camp when he glimpsed the horseman striking up one of the bluff trails. He guessed his destination to be Brass's camp and rode to intercept him.

The man didn't appear, so he turned and hunted back and forth across coulees and river bluffs. He'd about given up; then he dropped over the brink of a steep bank and was almost atop him.

Blair had spurred his horse to a stiff trot and was so intent on something ahead he wasn't even aware of John's sudden appearance.

A wolf howl cut the night, and Blair reined in with a sudden twist of his bridle. He was still watching. The howl came again, and obviously he'd been waiting for it. He cupped his hands to answer, and at that instant came his first realization that someone was riding up behind him.

He turned with one hand darting toward his gun, but the movement froze when he saw who it was.

'Why, sure. Take it easy,' John drawled. 'Keep ca'm, and live long. And answer that wolf just like ye intended. It's a language I always been interested in.'

'What are you talking about?' he asked in a voice drawn high and taut.

'You know, I reckon. That weren't a real wolf. Leastwise not the four-legged kind. So you answer.'

John was a little way off, partly hidden by the buffalo berry bushes that choked the bottom of the wash, but not far enough so Blair dared brave his Navies. So Blair said, 'All right,' and cupped his hands to cry, *'How-how-wh-o-o'* in fair imitation of a timber wolf.

The answer came almost instantly, and this time John guessed its distance as half a mile.

'Who be it?' he asked.

Blair was trying to think of a lie and couldn't. His face looked taut and hollow. He shook his head and spoke in a voice little better than a hard whisper.

'I don't know.'

'Don't ye, now? You're lying to me. You're lying because you think I'd kill ye if ye told the truth. That's Brass, or some of his rattlesnakes, and I dare say you're meetin' 'em hyar according to plan.'

Blair licked his lips. He kept looking from John's face to that right-hand Navy and back again. He made a dry swallow. Finally he got hold of himself enough to smile. 'You seem to be pretty smart.'

'A lone wolf has to be smarter'n a pack, and that goes for humans, too, I reckon. Now you already used up all the time I got to spare, so you answer quick, and you answer true. From hyar on I'm giving you no second chance. It's Brass's renegades, ain't it?'

He looked sick from fear. 'Yes.'

'How many be they?'

'I don't know.' He thought John's hand was moving to draw, and cried, 'I don't. Kill me, but I can't tell you what I don't know!'

'You guess how many.'

'Twenty.'

'The whole pack of 'em! What they figuring on?'

'To burn out the camp, I suppose.'

'So tonight's the night. And you were going to lead 'em in! Why, so ye will. So we will. Sure, we'll *both* lead 'em in, and just so's they won't lack for excitement, we'll manage to let Jim Swing and his sentries know a little bit ahead o' time.' He spat a stream of tobacco juice, indicating the little hills where the renegades waited.

'All right, you signal 'em to come along.'

'It won't work. They'll see I'm not alone and cut loose–'

'Then don't let 'em see. I'll keep hyar in the shadow, and you ride for'ard. Can't tell, Blair, you play along with me, doing just what I say, and it might be you'd come out o' this all in one chunk, without leaks. But if ye try anything shifty I promise to fill ye so full o' lead they won't bury ye at all; they'll stake a claim on ye, and ship your carcass to the smelter in Swansea, Wales.'

'All right.' His voice sounded dry and thirsty. 'Don't get ringy. I'll do what you say.'

The wolf signal sounded again, this time closer, apparently from a man concealed beyond a sandstone reef that broke the crest of a hilltop about four hundred yards south.

John said, 'Ride yonder. Slow. That's it. Little further. Thar, that's good. They'll see ye thar. Now you give 'em the high sign, and, by grab, they better follow.'

Blair took off his hat, lifted it high, and

swung it in repeated sweeps from side to side. 'Hi-ya!' he cried. 'Hi-ya!' came his answer.

He reined around with his hat still high, and rode back at a gallop with John swinging through the brush beside him.

'That'll bring 'em?' John asked when a shoulder of ground hid them from sight.

'I did my best.'

'You keep right on doing your best!'

They headed up the bottom of a feeder gully, across a ridge, and were close to the river.

John had his right-hand Navy out now. 'Wait for 'em!'

Blair was twenty-five yards off, staying in sight while John kept in shadow. He pulled up, still not daring to make a break for it. 'I'm waiting.'

Over the breathing of his horse John could hear the distant drum of hoofs. There were twenty, easily enough, perhaps closer to thirty.

'You git that hat in the air and keep 'em coming.'

'All right,' Blair said through his teeth.

'Then you stick with me down this draw to the cutbanks. That'll put us nigh over camp.'

Blair swung his hat again and was down the coulee at a gallop with John at his heels.

They struck a trail, deep-pounded by buffalo for a thousand years. It took them down through cutbanks, then it turned sharply between walls of brush.

Suddenly the camp was in view, less than half a mile away.

John called, 'Wait!' and pulled up again until he heard them. He slapped the pommel of his saddle and cried, 'By dang, it worked! Blair, you ain't going to stand very high with them renegades in another five minute. But we got to ride. We got to git that camp roused up for the party.'

They hit open ground at a gallop. It was slightly downhill to the camp. At the right was a tiny gully where Jim Swing had his sentry post. Just outside pistol range John drew up and called, 'Jim! Jim Swing!'

He heard the man breathe out hard and say, 'John? What the devil! I was about ready to cut loose at ye.'

'It's me and Blair, and we got the whole legion o' hell on our heels. Brass and his varmints. Git for camp and git thar on the run. Have your men betwixt the two draws. They'll follow us down in squaw-gun range.'

He still couldn't see Swing, but he could hear the rapid downhill thud of his boots as he ran toward camp.

A second sentry called to Jim Swing from a distance, 'Jim? What's wrong, anyhow?'

John wanted to answer him but he didn't dare. The renegades were too close. Calling now might have alarmed them.

He noticed Blair had come to a stop, and

swung a Navy to cover him. 'Don't spile it now!'

Blair cried, 'They'll hear you! You don't dare pull the trigger.'

It was true and they both knew it. Blair dug his spurs and wheeled his horse. He was off at a run. The sentry, now alarmed, fired at him.

It was a wild blast in the night. The renegades were just coming up, and the bullet rattled branches over their heads.

One of the renegades, taut from excitement, fired back. The bullet narrowly missed Blair and he shouted, 'No! It's me! Blair!'

He was too late. A volley of gunfire met him and smashed him back, over the rump of his horse, and he hit the earth with arms flung wide.

Rambo's voice, 'You damn fools, it was *him* – Blair!'

Shep– 'C'mon. We can't help it now. Downhill before this shootin' brings 'em out like hornets.'

They burst from the brush and were downhill at a gallop. Gunfire met them. At first a scattering of shots from far out. The renegades whooped and fired back.

'Hunt your holes, hyar we come!' Rambo shouted.

For a few seconds John was caught between them. He turned the gunpowder sharply. The brink of a dry wash opened before him. The ground was soft and crumbly. It gave way and rolled in a cloud over him. The gunpowder lost footing and was on his side. Bareback, John had no trouble rolling free. He let the animal go and ran down the brushy bottom.

The draw broadened and he could see half-clothed men hurrying uphill from the shanties.

'Yonder in the draws! Let 'em ride between ye!'

They couldn't hear him, but Jim Swing and Pike Wilbur knew what to do anyway, and the attackers suddenly found themselves caught in a deadly cross fire.

There was a mêlée of plunging horses as some of them tried to go on and others to retreat. Men were down, being trampled.

There'd been little planning in the first place and none at all now. It was every man for himself in the scramble for survival.

'Down the cutbanks!' Pike Wilbur was shouting. 'Stevens, get your men over that way. Cut 'em down when they try to make the trail!'

Half a dozen of the raiders turned on the gallop and were almost atop John's position in the draw. They were met by the blast from both Navies, and changed direction. One of them, wounded, made a grab for the neck of his horse and stayed with him over a bulge of ground, out of sight into darkness.

Shep, together with seven or eight of his men who had stayed behind, were now laying down a frenzied barrage of rifle and pistol fire from the edge of the brush. It saved the main group of his raiders. In five minutes the battle died down to long-range shooting, then that became infrequent.

Comanche John finished reloading his Navies, and hunted for Pike Wilbur. He was down at the camp, applying splints to a wounded man's leg. John chuckled with pleasure when he saw it was Wilcoxson.

'Why ye go to the bother? I'd take *that* one out and shoot him. When a man ain't got better brains, than a mule I say he ought to get the treatment o' one.'

Wilcoxson was blind from pain, but the sound of John's voice made him come around. 'You kilt poor Blair, didn't ye?'

'No, I didn't. His own men kilt him. Shep and his renegades.'

Wilbur said, 'What do you mean about Blair?'

'I mean he was a spy. A dirty, belly-crawlin' spy. I thought it was him and followed from Brass's, and it was. Only Wilcoxson, thar, fooled me, telling Blair's lie, saying he'd got in before midnight.'

Wilcoxson writhed from the pain of his bullet-shattered leg, but he still could say, 'He wasn't a spy. *You're* the spy. Way down by the shanties we could hear you yelling to them raiders, trying to lead 'em down on us so they could massacree us all.'

Jim Swing came up with his face streaked black from dirt and powder smoke. 'That's fool talk,' he said. 'John led 'em down hyar so's we could whipsaw 'em.'

The Californy men believed it, but the Pike's Peakers doubted. They were suspicious of John. Now they were suspicious of everyone. They held a meeting inside their biggest bunkhouse and came out grim and set-jawed, saying nothing. If it hadn't been for half of their wages being held till the completion of the boat, they'd have quit and gone downriver at dawn.

Chapter Eight

Devil's Deadfall

The Parson was a happy man next morning, reading at length from his tattered Bible over the single grave of seven dead renegades. At intervals he paused to point out their bullet-riddled bodies and expostulate on the wages on sin.

'Amen!' Comanche John intoned, laying hands on a shovel when it was over. 'Short and full o' bullet lead is the life o' man when he takes to riding down the black gulch o' sin, especially if he ain't mighty fast on the grab and twice as accurate.'

Work was resumed on the boat. Extra guards patrolled the rims, but the Pike's Peakers were still morose and suspicious. After talking with them, the Parson found Wilbur and said, 'Might be you could pay 'em a little on account and cheer 'em up.'

'If I paid them the half they have coming they'd leave before sundown. Maybe they'll quit me anyhow.'

The Pike's Peakers had another powwow after grub pile that noon, and Hames, the sawyer, a little, quick-tempered man, came up to the house where Wilbur and John were eating.

'I want to see you about our pay,' he said, peering into the shaded interior.

Wilbur said, 'You'll get it when it's due.'

'How do we know that?'

John said, 'How d'you know you'll live till sundown?'

Wilbur quieted him and walked outside. 'Hames, you're generally pretty level-headed. What's got into you, anyhow?'

'I'll tell you what – we been hearing things, and there's them that say you'll never get steam power in this boat, and even if you do you'd never dare sail it into American Flag with Captain Brass top dog in the town.'

'Who's been saying those things?'

'Never mind who said 'em, they're being said.'

Comanche John was outside, wiping grease from his whiskers with the back of his hand. 'Waal, next time ye hear it said, tell him we'll finish this boat and put power in her if we have to carry the engine upriver from St Louis on our backs. And when we get 'er installed we'll sail into American Flag, and if Cap'n Brass and his yella Yankee vigilance committee get in the way we'll mow 'em down like we did that renegade bunch he turned loose on us last night.'

When Hames was gone, John said to Pike, 'I reckon them punkin rollers don't think you got the money.'

'It *is* going to stretch me pretty tight – paying them and getting my steam-power equipment from the Far West Company up at Benton.'

The Pike's Peakers went back to work, but something was afoot, and John suspected there was an element among them who'd be willing to work for Brass if he guaranteed them an advance in wages. Failure of one raid wouldn't stop the fellow. He'd bounce back with something else. There was no way he could stop the Pike's Peakers if they wanted to leave, but he might stop Brass getting an emissary inside to encourage them.

He rode out along the rims. A stormy

darkness settled. There were gusty wind and lightning, but no rain. He slept in an abandoned wickiup, got up at dawn, and ate hard biscuit and jerky from his saddlebag. The day was cold for the season. Almost a feel of snow in the air. He slept again at the wickiup, ate the last of his jerky, and drifted back. It had been dark for three hours when he sighted the home camp.

There was still a fire burning. It made him wary, suspicious of visitors, those Benton vigilantes, maybe. He took one of the little-used trails downhill until a sentry hailed him. It was an undersized Californy man by the name of Hagen.

'Something wrong?' John asked, jerking his head at the camp.

'What kind of eye for trouble you got?'

'I'm alive and past forty. I got a good eye for trouble. Gen'rally that fire's down to coals an hour ago.'

'Reckon Mrs Coppens kept it going just for you.'

'Ye mean she's waitin' for me?'

'Why, yes. So I hear.'

John let out a whoop and gave the pony his head. The pony, scenting the home corral, was downhill at a gallop. John hit the clearing and shouted, 'Yipee, hyar I be, Mrs Coppens. Come on out of that shanty. I can ride like a cocklebur and sing like a wolf, and, by grab, this is my night to howl.'

Mrs Coppens was dressed and watching for him. She ran outside, holding her long dress away from her feet. 'John! Listen to me, John!'

He reined around so sharply the pony almost lost footing. Then the startled animal commenced to buck. John stuck with him, but he lost his hat and one of his Navies. 'Hyar I be, Mrs Coppens. A man like ye come across a thousand mile of dry-bone prairie to find. I'm tougher'n a bull buffalo and wilder'n a Blackfoot on free likker. Crawl in your holes, you Pike's Peak punkin rollollers and don't bother me when I'm talkin' to my gal, because I ain't shot a man since day before yestiddy and I can't abide the sight o' Yankees.'

'Stop it!' she was screaming. 'This is no time for foolery–'

'This ain't foolery, Mrs Coppens. I'm a ring-tailed roarer and I ain't combed the ticks out o' my whiskers since I left Yuba Gulch.' He got his pony quieted and made a considerable show of retrieving his hat and Navy without leaving his saddle. 'Reckon ye never had a man around the house doing a trick like *that*. By dang, Mrs Coppens, one o' these days I hanker to settle down, and you're the kind o' woman I want.'

'I tell ye for the last time to quit acting like drunken fool. They left not three hours after you did. Should have been back last night.

136

He promised they'd be back by then. And when the meat hunter was down past the falls last night he heard gunfire. Lots of gunfire.'

'Who you talking about?'

'Mr Wilbur and the Parson, of course. They went to Benton to pay money on that engine. Lucas went with 'em, and that no-account half-breed called Pete Rock. Shifty-eyed redskin, won't even come to church. Knew they shouldn't have gone with him.'

John started to laugh off her apprehension, but Dallas came outside and said, 'I'm worried, too, John. He really meant it when he promised to get back.'

Mrs Coppens said, 'He had money along. A heap o' money. That's one of the things that worries me.' She gave John a long look. 'What with road agents skulking the trails, waiting for honest folk.'

'Don't cast that camp-meetin' eye at me, woman. I'm innocent as a babe unborn.'

'Ye got a heart as black as the knave o' spades. Ye ain't got learnin' and ye ain't got calluses, and I say a man that don't have one or t'other is living on the windward side o' the Ten Commandments. But enough o' this. I'll reform ye with an ax when the time comes right, but right now I got need of ye. You git yourself a fresh horse saddled and find out what's wrong.'

'I'm hungry.'

'By the time you got that horse caught and

saddled, I'll have victuals for ye.'

John found his gunpowder and swapped saddles. Back at the house Mrs Coppens had a plate of warmed-over buffalo stew ready. He ignored the fork that went with it, and ate it with his bowie knife.

She said, 'Maybe ye better rouse Jim Swing and some of the boys.'

'Need 'em on guard duty. No'm, I ain't one o' those single-shot fighting men, Mrs Coppens. I'll handle this thing all alone.'

'What if them Brass renegades attacked 'em?'

'Why, if they did, they did. It's over and done with. They're either dead or captured or on the high lope. It wouldn't help to have extra men along.'

'Amen! Ye don't think they'd shoot the Parson?'

'After the trouble that old buzzard's caused, Brass would shoot him and carve a double-deep notch.'

John finished the stew without leaving the saddle and handed the empty plate back to her. He headed out of camp and was just cantering up the hill trail when Dallas called to him.

'Yeah, I was expectin' ye.' He watched without enthusiasm while she rode toward him, but he didn't remonstrate. There was no changing her mind once she'd set it on something. 'Likely we just got a long ride ahead and nothing but sore bones at t'other end of it.'

'That's all right. I want to visit Benton anyway. They have an opera house there now, you know.'

'Fact is, I didn't. Somehow, I ain't been keeping up on my opery o' late.' He noticed she'd slid a sawed-off shotgun in the scabbard beneath her saddle. 'Must be you have a mind to shoot up that opery house.'

Rain had been threatening since sundown. It was quite dark on the prairie except when lightning came, revealing the country with brief, bluish light, and afterward it would seem darker than ever. They rode along the rims until they sighted Brass's boat camp. There were a couple of big bonfires burning and torches on standards lighted the carpentry sheds.

John said, 'Must be working night and day. I do believe that tall bushway means business.'

'Of course he means business. If he can't stop us from finishing the boat, he intends to beat us and be the first to establish a steam-packet service between American Flag and the Falls. That would give him inside track on the mail franchise, and whoever gets the mail will get most of the gold shipments and the insured express.'

'Union skulduggery.'

'But he won't be first. *We'll* be first. Then

we'll have the government backing. It won't be Union skulduggery then.'

'Don't put too much faith in the North, gal, because the words is on the wall; they're writ in blood ten feet high, and they all say that old Robbie Lee is about to knock the stuffing out of U. S. Grant.'

John left her at the rims and rode toward Brass's camp, but workmen were everywhere, and he didn't risk approaching the cabins. When he got back a fine rain was falling.

'See anything?' she asked.

'Horses and corrals, plenty of 'em, but not many saddles around. Maybe he fired them renegades, and maybe not. Best we drift toward Benton and look around.'

They crossed Sun River. Beyond were benches and dry lake beds, with here and there a deep, steep-sided coulee slicing toward the river.

It became quiet, with the electrical storm swinging toward the eastern mountains and only a soft patter of rain.

A group of horsemen were caught against the sky line by a particularly long flash of lightning. John said, 'Hold it!' and grabbed Dallas's bridle. 'Better git in this dry wash.'

'What's the matter?'

'Why, nothing yet. We'll see.'

They sat quite still for a minute, then a voice came to them, a treble voice – Captain Brass.

140

'Him!' She pulled around, angry that he wanted her to hide.

'Listen here, I don't like sneaking away from him any more'n you do, and take my word for it I'd of punched holes through him already if it hadn't been for making it tougher on young Wilbur.'

They could hear other voices from their place in the dry wash, a jingle of bridle links, sometimes the clatter of a steel shoe on stone.

The riders were strung out in two or three groups. A voice was raised, saying, 'Dammit, Dillman, quit ragging me. I didn't throw the gun away. I lost it. You lost plenty o' things along the way. You lost your guts some place—'

'Don't talk too much; you might end up with a bullet in your mouth.'

The voices, still querulous, became distant.

John said, 'Nice, friendly boys, them renegades. From the sound, maybe things didn't go off too well.'

'Where do you think they've been?'

'It ain't been to a temperance meetin'. Only thing we can do is back-trail and see.'

Their tracks were easy to follow across the rain-softened clay of the prairie, but after about five miles they faded. John dismounted and walked ahead, tracing them down a coulee, up the other side. Rain was coming harder. It soaked his black slouch hat and ran in a tiny stream around the brim. Finally he stopped and used a stick of sage to dig mud from his boots.

'What do you think?' Dallas asked.

'Why, we be whipsawed on this trail with the rain on one side and the dark on t'other. Can't track 'em any further without light, and by dawn the rain will have all the sign washed away. Best we can do is make a guess and gamble on it. From here I'd say they turned off the stage road whar she crossed that big sand-rock coulee.'

It rained steadily throughout the three hours it took them to reach the road. Tiny streams were running along its twin ruts where it slanted down into the coulee.

'Anyhow, this rain softens up my chawin' tobaccy,' John said.

There was a log shed in the coulee bottom, a warm-up spot for stage passengers during cold weather, and back of it a small corral where extra horses were kept to help on the long drag uphill when the snow was deep. All empty tonight.

'Brass own this coach?' he asked.

'No. This is Diamond B Bettenhoff Steam Transportation Company. Brass operates his coaches from American Flag and Last Chance south to Salt Lake City. He has an agreement with Bettenhoff. He doesn't compete with their coaches and they ship all their freight on his wagons.'

The road stayed with the coulee bottom for a quarter mile, then it made two switchbacks in climbing the north side. At the rims they heard the clatter and creak of an approaching stagecoach and drew off to one side while it went by.

John looked at the weaving rear of it, the boot jammed full of baggage, and shot a contemptuous stream of tobacco juice.

'Shotgun guard nappin'. Thinks that gun's a prop to hold him up. Driver full o' trade likker. One man with a sawed-off down by that jackknife turn could take 'em clean as the Parson's conscience.'

'You wouldn't rob a coach, would you, John?' She was watching him with a slight smile.

'Me! I should say I wouldn't. Not a down-going one, especially. Why, likely they ain't anything on that mud wagon except Yankee greenbacks, and take my word for it, Jeff Davis ain't going to pay one cent on the dollar for 'em when the war's over. Anyhow, I'm getting a bit old for coach robbin'. I hanker for the quiet life.' Then he added, quite irrelevantly, 'Share and share alike's my motto.'

'Does that include another man's money?'

'Child, you listen to me. Greed's the root o' evil, and gold is the apple that grows on the tree. Worse'n pizen them apples be, if ye don't know how to use 'em. Look at what happened to the children o' Israel when they quit farming the soil and lit out on that gold rush looking for some nugget as big as a heifer calf. Everything was quiet and decent, and soon as they hit the color thar they were with a couple o' boom camps called Soda and Gamorrah. These camps weren't hyar, or in Californy, even, but some place else and before my time, but I've heered the Parson tell about 'em and from what he said I'd guess that Soda was worse'n Last Chance and Gamorrah was nigh onto as bad as Bannack. Well, these children o' Israel, who were really the Pike's Peakers o' that day, had a wagon cap'n by the name o' Moses. By grab, thar's a man I'd like to known. He was like Jeff Davis and Stonewall Jackson and the Parson all rolled into one. He got 'em over a country that was so rough and dry it'd make the road from Hoss Crick to the Humboldt look like Illini. He suffered and slaved for them Israelites, and then when he come back and saw what a wing-ding they'd gone off on, on account o' a few pokes of the heavy color he cut loose and *did* the feathers fly! Ripped through 'em like the Alabama light horse at Shiloh. O' course them children o' Israel weren't any better or worse than any bunch o' stampeders. It just shows what'll happen to ordinary folk when they git the stampede fever. So when I see a man with too much gold for his good I lift it.

144

Hard to tell how many I saved off the rocky path o' perdition. Little enough thanks I ever got for it. But for that matter, little enough got Moses.' John thought he could see amazement in her face, and said, with a careless gesture that sent rain streaming from the gutter of his turned-up hatbrim, 'Oh. I'm up on the Bible, all right. That's what I got from shacking up with a sky pilot. I heered that old rooster preach till I know 'er from Beer to Beersheba and back to the case cyards.'

After long, silent travelling along the road, John pulled up and said, 'You say something?'

'No.' She'd heard it, too. 'It sounded like a groan. Off that way, toward the river.'

John cupped his hands and said, 'Hey, thar!'

It surprised him, to get back an answer almost instantly. 'John! Did I hear your voice, John?'

'Damme, it's the Parson.' And he shouted, 'Yes, ye heered my voice. Whar be ye, anyhow?'

He rode off with the high sagebrush slapping his stirrups. Through rainy darkness he could see nothing.

'Parson, keep shouting, otherwise I'll get turned about. It's black as the inside of a mine.'

He hunted through sage and finally caught

sight of the Parson, lean and bedraggled, staggering.

'Whar's your horse?'

The Parson's right arm hung limp inside a sleeve turned heavy from blood. He'd lost his hat. His long gray hair was plastered to his skull, tangled with twigs.

'Thank the Lord ye heered me, John. I lay thar thinking I'd never lift leg again, praying that succor would come, and blessed be the Book, here ye are.'

John got to the ground in time to grab the Parson as he lurched to fall. He lifted him in his arms, noticing how little meat there was on his old bones, and tramped a place to lay him in a big sage clump.

'Hyar, you lie still. You took a bullet, and your arm's broke. Tain't a new wound, either. When'd you get this, Parson, yestiddy? I guess you had a dispute with Brass and his renegades.'

'It war them, all right,' the Parson whispered. 'But they didn't kill me. Bet they didn't! I'm tough as an old sage turkey. I'll get 'long. You leave me be and ride yonder. They's them as needs help worse.'

Dallas was bending over him, saying, 'Pike? Tell me – how about Pike?'

'Shot. Shot bad. No, he ain't dead. Lucas, he's the one they killed. Him and Pete Rock. Pete crawled off somewhere. I shouted and called to him, but he never answered.'

146

Dallas had hold of his shoulder. 'Where is he? Where did you leave him? Answer me!'

'Yonder. I don't know how far. There was two coulees. They run together. I–'

'Let him rest a while, gal.'

She stepped back. 'I'm sorry.'

The Parson opened his eyes and went on in his wispy voice, 'Brass and his renegades, it was. Twenty of 'em. Maybe more'n twenty of 'em. Bullets. They came from every which way.'

'Take it ca'm, Parson. Just talk slow.'

'T'was last night. No. Night before last. We started out for Benton. They jumped us and we run for it. Took off down a coulee. Come to a cabin and holed up in it. All day and them killers shootin' down on us from the cutbanks. That's when Lucas got killed. Bullet hit him here.' He struck his stomach. 'Came dark and we tried to sneak off. Shot our horses, they did, but we got off afoot. River too far. I got Pike up the side, hid underneath the rimrocks. All day without water. Thar he was, calling for a drink, and I had to keep his mouth gagged so's them killers wouldn't hear. They kept riding back and forth looking for us. Sometimes they was so close I could smell the stinkin' sweat of their clothes.'

'When'd ye start out?'

'At dark.'

Talk had exhausted him. He lay back with

147

his eyes closed. He took a deep breath that whistled as it left, and his face looked sharp and lifeless.

Dallas gave a start and said, 'Is he–'

'No, he's alive.' John listened to his heart. 'It's still bumping his ribs good and hard. They don't give up the spirit very easy when they're ornery like the Parson. He's tough as jerky out of a Jan'wary buffalo. But we'll have to do something about that arm.'

It had been shattered midway between elbow and shoulder, and he'd lost considerable blood. John drew his bowie and carefully cut the shirt away.

'Ye see? Every time he moves them bones spring apart, and it starts the blood again. I hate to mention it, gal, but one time on the Green River I was with a wagon train that got jumped by Cheyennes and nigh onto all the wagons burned, but the women carried bandages right on their persons. Called 'em petticoats.'

Dallas stepped out of sight beyond the horses and returned in a couple of minutes with the desired garment. The petticoat was natural-bleach linsey, ideal for a bandage.

He started with pads, on which he scraped tobacco from his plug. These he pressed on both sides of the wound and bound tight. He shattered the stock of his rifle for splints, and ended by tying the arm close to the body.

Dallas was growing ill from worry. 'How

about Pike? Do you really think he's alive?'

The Parson whispered, 'He'll live. I don't know why I'm sure of it, but I am. With your prayers, he'll live.'

Chapter Nine

Outdrawed With Two Sixes

Rain and darkness made one section of the prairie look like the next. The Parson, mounted on the gunpowder and tied to the saddle, kept weaving, jerking awake every four or five minutes to say, 'There! That way!' Each time pointing a different direction.

John walked ahead. In spite of darkness he managed to keep to the Parson's meandering tracks. After an hour of it he stopped to scan the country.

'Daylight'll catch us and still we'll be nowhere at this rate. We better make a guess at it and cut across. I have an idee what coulee he's talking about.'

The Parson woke up and tossed his good arm back in the direction they'd just come from.

'That way!'

'Sure, Parson. We're going thar now.'

Rain diminished to a thin drizzle, but

there was no break in the clouds overhead. As a rule the gray-white gumbo of the prairie reflected light even on the darkest night so that the broad features of the country were discernible, but rain had now turned the ground amorphous black.

A coulee opened in front of them, and John shook the Parson to wake him. 'Here, Parson. You wake up and have a look.'

The Parson sat a long time and said, 'I can't be sure. Things look different somehow. Be those cliffs? That'd be right. And there'd be three sandrock pillars where two coulees came together.'

'We better go down,' John said. 'I wouldn't want to be caught on the sky line if Brass left a few snipers behind.'

The coulee was steep, but grass had taken root, and it gave them footing to the bottom. There it was choked by rose and bullberry bushes. Hard going. The sides steepened with rock breaking through, forming continuous cliffs. The coulee broadened, and ahead, silhouetted against the sky, were three pillars of stone.

The Parson jerked back suddenly and said in his parroty voice, 'It's them!'

His voice startled a horse somewhere in the blackness ahead of them. The animal took a single crashing leap through brush. He was tied, by the sound of him, and he hit the end of his halter and fell. Next second the night was sliced by a streak of burning powder with concussion following it.

A bullet struck rock with a ping and whined as it flew away.

Dallas reined hard and drew her pistol, but John took a long stride and had her by the wrist.

'No. It might be *him*. Wilbur.'

'No it ain't,' said the Parson. 'Nary a bullet we had left.'

Echo was gone from the air and silence pressed in hard. The rain had all stopped. On the slight breeze came an odor of burned powder.

'You wait,' John muttered, and moved forward.

He didn't draw. He seemed slouched and careless, but he walked without rattling a pebble with his boots or scraping a single branch with his clothes.

He could sense movement in the night. A rock started somewhere. It slid downhill and ended with a whisper in dry weeds.

'Blakely!' a man called. He was somewhere among the rimrocks, maybe seventy-five yards off. John had heard the voice before – at Piegan and again at Brass's camp. 'What's wrong down there, Blakely?'

It was Blakely who had fired the shot. He knew better than to answer. The horse moved, stamped. Closer than John expected. He stopped and was still except for his hands, which kept moving back and forth an inch or so, palms down on the sodden fabric of his homespun pants. 'Blakely!' the man bellowed. 'Dammit, answer me.'

Blakely moved, and at that instant he and John saw each other.

Blakely was holding a pistol in his hand. He spun with it, but John leaned back, upholstering both Navies with a deft movement that had become reflex to him. Blakely was hit by two pistol balls and smashed back. He pulled the trigger and fired overhead. For a second his eyes were wide with shock. Then he went limp and crumpled, to the ground.

'Blakely!' the man called again.

John walked on, the smoking Navies in his hands, trying to see the man on the rims above. He spat and said, 'Hyar! Nothing to git upset about. I just shot a rattler.'

'You ain't Blakely!'

'Could be I ain't. Could be I'm Comanche John on the hunt for bushwhackers so yella-bellied they lay in wait to finish off wounded men.'

He waited for an answer. There was none. Only a horse galloping off. He chuckled and rammed the Navies back. Dallas and the Parson came up and stopped when they saw Blakely's body.

John said, 'Thar's one to pay off for Lukas. Maybe I'll git some luck and bag one for that wounded flipper o' yours, Parson.'

'I ain't vengeful. Fills my heart with sorrow to see a man go down with his boots on and no repentance in his soul.'

'An eyetooth for an eyetooth, that's what Leviticus said, and as for repenting, I dare guess *this* one did a lot of it in a short time when he saw he was outdrawed.'

John untied the dead man's horse, talking in an easy voice to keep the animal quieted down. 'Easy, boy. You made a good trade in owners.' He shortened the stirrups, and the horse stood still with his flanks trembling while John mounted. 'Now, Parson, you lead us straight on and we'll take care of such trouble as presents herself.'

He didn't expect trouble. No man gunning for money likes to go up against the long odds, so those snipers that Brass had left were probably high-tailing it for the upcountry already.

'Those your pillars, Reverend?'

The Parson jerked awake. 'Yes. He'll be yonder, in them undercut caves, unless they already found him.'

The coulees here had cut deeply through prairie on their way to the river. Often they branched and reunited, leaving island masses with sides of vertical stone and dirt with the prairie grass still growing at their tops. Fallen rock made the going tough.

After long wandering the Parson stopped and called above, 'Pike! Pike, boy! Answer me. This is the Parson.'

After the passage of a quarter minute taut with apprehension a voice responded, 'Yeah! Here.' It was scarcely recognizable as Pike Wilbur's. 'Got to have a drink.'

Despite rain, there was no water for him. They left their horses and climbed afoot. The cave was actually a deep slot where shale had been eroded beneath a stratum of more resistant sandstone. It was littered with twigs and bones that had been accumulated by pack rats through many years.

Dallas went in on hands and knees, saying, 'Pike!'

There was a catch in her breath when she saw him. 'You're all right?'

It was a foolish question. She knew he was wounded, scarcely alive. John crawled in with her and helped her lift him outside. His eyes were open, but he only half compre-hended what was happening.

Dallas held his head in her lap while John had a look at his wounds.

'He tooken a couple, all right. One in the ribs and one low down. That's the bad one.'

'You don't think he'll—'

'Gal, I'd like to make ye feel good, but it wouldn't be fair. I seen men shot this way before, and it's just like win or lose on the faro box. Half and half, like that, with always the splits in favor of the house man. We got to get him out o' hyar and to Benton.'

154

He wasn't a light man, and it was a struggle getting him to the rims without opening his abdominal wound again. While John brought the horses up, Dallas pulled handfuls of wet sage leaves and bathed his dirt-crusted face and chest.

Somehow they managed to keep him on horseback for ten miles, to the stage station at Gros Ventre Butte.

The station keeper, an unwashed old squawman named Dad Faseen, hitched a team of broncs to his buckboard and drove him to Benton.

It was midafternoon with the sun shining hot through the washed atmosphere when they dropped down the steep road to the river town. Originally it had been built to supply fur traders who braved the dangerous country of the Blackfeet, but since John White's discovery of gold at Bannack, and subsequent strikes at Alder, Last Chance, Confederate, and American Flag, it had boomed, multiplying its size many times in the course of a couple of years until now it boasted upward of two thousand inhabitants.

A steamboat with black pitch smoke still rolling from her twin chimneys had just come to rest against one of the docks, after completing the long voyage from St Louis, and with most of the town down to greet her, scant attention was paid to the wounded man, or to Comanche John who

155

rode behind the buckboard with his hat pulled low over his eyes.

Dad Faseen drew up in front of a low log building and helped carry Wilbur inside, then he went in search of the doctor who proved to be a young German, clumsy at English but marvellously dextrous at probing for the bullet.

Dallas watched him, her face pale beneath the tan, until he was through and had the wounds bandaged.

'Will he live?'

'*Ja* – maybe. In this climate. Here it is hot, pure. Since I am here, of these wounds' – he pressed his abdomen – 'two of three have lived. That is goot. In some climates, not half. There is no hemorrhage. I think, with a long rest he will live.'

There were hotels, but men slept four together and paid to pitch their bedrolls in the halls. The doctor let Pike Wilbur stay in one of the tiny rooms behind his office, and he fixed a cot so Dallas could be close to nurse him. John spent the night in a hay shed and arose at dawn.

He came in the back way and saw Dallas.

'How is he?'

'He spent a good night.'

'That's the answer – rest, and the care of a woman. You stay with him. Best I git back to camp. Has he talked any?'

'Sometimes he's delirious. He talks about

156

the boat, and about the money.'

'Brass got away with it?'

'I suppose. He had it in a saddlebag. The horse was shot from under him. They wounded him at the same time. He can't even remember getting to the cave, let alone what happened to the money.'

'What's due on that machinery?'

'I don't know the amount. He paid a fourth with the order. He was to pay another fourth when he took it, and the last half was to be secured by a mortgage due next June.'

'You see that Far West Company about it. Mightn't be too healthy for me prowling town, with them vigilantes having their ropes out. Send the Parson when he's able. I better git back and make them Pike's Peakers hump.'

He rode down on the river camp and found things almost at a standstill.

'Git off your haunches,' he roared. 'Git that lumber moving. Whar's the planking crew?'

The Pike's Peakers responded by holding one of their interminable powwows. John went to the cookhouse and told Mrs Coppens to rest up for the day. At sundown there was no supper, and when they came around with their tin plates to learn the reason it was John who greeted them.

'Boys, it grieves me to say that the pot's empty. By grab, I see no reason why Mrs

157

Coppens shouldn't take the day to rest up like everybody else. What's more, she's taking the morning off, and the state o' your bellies come dinnertime depends on the amount o' work I see done.'

They went breakfastless in the morning and put in a grudging half day's work. After that, John gave commands and saw them obeyed. Things went along with scarcely a hitch. The planking was completed, and he put the carpentry crew inside the hull to construct engine and boiler supports and lay the deck planks.

The Parson came down on the Benton stage as far as the ford of the Sun and walked the intervening seven miles despite his bullet-shattered arm.

Mrs Coppens had him in bed with a hot sling made of tea, trade likker, and Watson's Reliable Pain Killer when John found him.

'How is he?' John asked, meaning Pike.

'Alive. First a good night, then a bad one. But I been praying. Both Dallas and I been praying.'

'See about the stream engine?'

'They won't release it without a full half in advance. But she 'lows she'll get it.'

John left him and went back to the boat. Most of the work was inside the hull now, so he split the crew into day and night shifts to relieve crowding. Two days later an epidemic of mountain fever swept camp.

Wilcoxson, up and around with the help of a willow crutch, claimed it was caused by breathing the night damp, and John, thinking maybe he was right, put them back to working single shift. No one was seriously ill, but the fever had way of leaving a man so weak that the mildest exertion brought sweat and attacks of the shakes.

John had to have additional help for the rough work, so he rode off to Last Chance where a Chinese labor broker 'sold' him fifteen coolies whom he brought back in a freight wagon. Dallas was standing by the whim saw waiting for him.

He asked about Pike, and she said he would recover, but that he'd be in bed for another three weeks. She hadn't been waiting to tell him about Pike, though. It concerned the machinery. She'd raised nearly four thousand dollars by selling some property that Faro Hill owned in Benton, but when she offered it to Severence, manager of Far West, he'd refused to deliver the machinery to her. He'd stalled, talked at length about the technicalities of their agreement, and had ended by refusing delivery unless the full price was paid over. When she reminded him that the full amount was not due until next summer, he'd bowed in his princely manner, still acting the part of the Southern gentleman, and said, 'You have recourse to the co'ts. Trouble is, miss, the co'ts aren't sure of themselves, either. Seems to be some question of jurisdiction at present being settled on the fields of Virginia.'

John blasted tobacco juice and said, 'That settles it. Tell ye, I'll get my Californy men together and ride yonder and *take* that engine.'

'Two tons of steel is a little harder to ride off with than a strongbox of gold.'

John stopped and said, 'Why, so it be.'

'All I can do is go back to American Flag.'

'And sell what you got there, too?'

'If I have to. Maybe there'll be enough in the faro bank.'

Chapter Ten

'Dirtier Business I Never See.'

John roped a fresh horse and went with her. At midnight they were at Frenchman's Roadhouse where a side trail branched off to ford the Missouri and wind through mountains to Confederate Gulch. There they ate, secured new mounts, and by steady riding, sighted American Flag early the next afternoon.

'Best you go yonder alone,' John said. 'Boys in thar might want to run races with me, and lately I've tooken a hanker for the quiet life.'

He took his ease in an abandoned prospector's shanty, napping, watching for her return. When she wasn't there by sundown he ate some cold-dummy he'd put in his saddlebag at the Frenchman's. He watched the lights come on in town and along the sluices that ran down from the placer cuts. The night was clear, and as it grew later he could hear sounds from the camp – the bang and clatter of construction, sometimes the tinkle of polka-time pianos. Finally he saw Dallas coming up the trail.

'I'm alone, John.'

'Sure, gal.' He put his Navies back in their holsters. 'You get that, heavy color?'

'No.'

'Should have known that place wouldn't run itself. What happened, them dealers raid the bank?'

'There's still money in the faro bank – if I could get it.' She dismounted and said, 'I *will* get it, tomorrow.'

'What do you mean, *tomorrow?* If there's money at the White Palace, by grab ye can take it any time ye like. Let's get back down thar and–'

'I don't want any trouble. Not if I can get it without trouble.'

'What happened?'

'That little rat-faced coward, Pillen. I never did trust him.' She was angry and it showed in the swing of her shoulders. 'I asked to open the strongbox, but Pillen claimed he couldn't because the key was locked in the safe at the express office. He went over after it, or *said* he was. Instead he must have run straight to Ox Farrell.'

'Who's Ox Farrell?'

'The town marshal. Anyway, I didn't see Pillen again, but Ox came half an hour later with a writ of attachment signed by Wendley, the government commissioner.'

'Now ain't that fancy! A gov'ment commissioner. Next thing they'll have congressmen and all that sort o' truck. By grab, what's the country coming to? Who is this commissioner, one o' Brass's yella-bellies?'

'I don't think so, I think he's honest. He issued the writ, but all I have to do is come around in the morning and show cause.'

'And he'll have ye showing cause from now till the thirty-second of Jan'wary.'

'No, he won't. I told Ox I was posting a miner's meeting. That scared him. The writ was for some debt I'd never heard tell of. They can't make it stick in front of a miner's meeting. You have to prove things to those fellows. They're getting fed up with Ox, and he knows it. If this gets out in the open they'll run him out of camp. Ox would have torn the writ up tonight, only he didn't dare without finding the commissioner, and he'd left for that new camp at Eldorado. I'll get in the strongbox tomorrow morning, all right.'

John grunted without conviction and freshened his chaw. 'Why, I sure enough hope you're right, gal.'

John had napped during the afternoon, so he stayed awake now, watching while Dallas slept on a heap of pine boughs in the cabin. It was about an hour past midnight when he heard the clanging of the fire bell down in camp. A red glow showed itself and climbed rapidly. He realized by its position that it was the White Palace.

'Dallas!' he called through the door. 'A dirtier piece o' business I never hope to see, but them Northerners are burning ye out.'

She ran outside and stood, wrapping her braided hair beneath her sombrero. The fire turned from ruddy red to bright yellow. It had burst through the roof. She didn't say a word, but her face looked thin, and her hand closed on the side-hammer pistol.

He took her arm and said, 'Gal, you been telling me not to start anything. Now I'll say it to you. You keep that gun in its scabbard.'

She tried to pull away. Then she stopped and said, 'All right. All right, let's get down there.'

John rode beside her as far as the main street, then he pulled in and let her ride ahead. A big crowd had gathered, and he kept to the back of it, still mounted, one leg crooked around the saddle horn, watching

163

the futile efforts of the volunteer fire crew with its new red pumping-wagon. Driven far away by the red heat of the blaze, they kept working the handles desperately without getting more than one gallon in ten to its intended destination.

With a thundering noise the big building collapsed in the middle, and the crew commenced playing their stream on smaller structures down the street; but that had no effect either, and an area one hundred feet long was flattened before the fire started to subside.

Dawn was coming then. The crowd thinned out. John rode around to the back, and sat in the shadow between two sheds that had escaped the fire. There he had a good view of the blackened rectangle where the White Palace had stood. Heaps of debris were still blazing, hiding the strongbox. He wondered where Dallas was. He hadn't seen her for an hour.

Horsemen were coming up on both sides of the sheds. He moved, and the Navies were out instinctively, but the men didn't see him. There were nine of them, masked by handkerchiefs draped from their hatbands, bodies covered by blankets, even the brands on the horses smeared with fresh mud. They had sawed-off shotguns ready.

Their approach had been unhurried, but quick. Well planned. Not a word spoken.

They ranged themselves around the back of the ruined building. One of them got down and walked directly into the hot embers, dragging a log chain with a hook end.

He had on heavy, water-soaked overboots. His trousers and blanket were wet, too. He kicked some charred wood aside, located the handle of the metal strongbox, hooked it. He signaled, and a second man, who had taken a dally around his saddle horn with the chain, skidded the strongbox out.

It all happened so quickly that spectators on the street side of the building wouldn't have realized what was going on had it not been for Dallas Hill, who came running and cried, 'The strongbox. Can't you see they're taking the strongbox?'

When no one made a move, she drew her pistol and fired. The bullet fell short, kicking a shower of coals. They were now roping the strongbox on a horse that had been equipped with a wooden packsaddle. She emptied the little gun at them, but the range was too long. In another fifteen seconds they were out of sight in the predawn darkness.

Comanche John had remained in the saddle only until he was sure of their purpose. He could have opened fire and got a few of them, but there were others at his back. Instead, he slid from the saddle and stepped inside the horse shed. There was enough fire glow coming through the door to reveal the harnesses, horse collars and blankets hanging on pegs along one wall. He pulled down one of the big gray blankets, slit it down the middle with his bowie, made an opening for his head, and draped it around him in the form of a poncho. He tied a handkerchief around his hat and stepped out just as they were roping down the strongbox.

They rode away not noticing that they now numbered ten instead of nine.

Once around the sheds, their leader, a tall man on a buckskin horse, spurred to a gallop. He led them uphill, around placer pits, then, with timber screening them from town, he slowed to a swift trot and pulled his mask off. Others did the same, all except for John, who dropped to the rear with the pack horse just ahead of him. For the moment, none of them noticed. It was still quite dark. He watched the side of the trail, hunting a place where he could grab the pack horse and make a break for it.

The short, oily-skinned man in front of John commenced pulling his blanket off. It was stitched in front, and he had to get it over his head. He turned, blowing his breath, and said, 'Ain't you hot, Eddie?'

'You say something to me?' someone said from up front.

The short man peered at John. 'Ain't you Eddie? Then who in hell are you?'

In answer, John whipped out a Navy with

one hand and grabbed the lead string of the pack horse with the other. He cried, 'Hi-ya!' dug the heels of his jackboots, and used a twist of his shoulder to send his pony downhill over the steep shoulder of the trail. The pack horse plunged close atop him.

For thirty yards it was a sliding descent. The short man fired one barrel of his sawed-off. Its close pattern tore the pine branches over John's head.

John hit the bottom of the steep drop and turned. The short man was swinging his gun for another shot. John fired as a matter of reflex, knocking him off his horse.

'No, not that way!' a man was shouting. 'Uphill! Cut him off uphill. It's the only way he can go.'

He could hear them crashing down through the scrub pine. Back of him were great angular boulders of slide rock. He had his choice of making the difficult climb back to the trail or of going straight ahead.

He chose the latter. For thirty yards he was in shadow, crossing ground heavily matted with pine needles. Suddenly there was slanting rock underfoot, and the pack horse fell.

John had dallied the lead string around his saddle horn, and the dally held, but the string itself snapped where it was tied to the halter. The pack horse got to its feet, walleyed from fright, and lunged back toward the trail.

A gun exploded so close in John's face he

could feel the whip and burn of powder. He turned and fired back. They were on all sides of him. No hope of recapturing the pack horse. He drew his other Navy, let out a war whoop, and rode into the midst of them.

'Ya-hoo! Ye ask who I was – I'm Comanche John. I'm a mangy old he-wolf from Yuba Gulch, and don't git in front of my guns or I'll turn ye so the hair side's in.'

His pony was blind-frightened from the flash and roar of gunfire. Firing with both hands, John still managed to stick in the saddle as the pony took him through timber, across rock and steep-slanting earth. When his guns were empty, he rammed them away and wheeled uphill. They were still shouting and firing behind him. Shooting at one another he guessed, for none of the bullets were close. Somebody was hit and cursing.

He found a trail and doubled back. A riderless horse came into view. For a second he thought luck had played into his hands, but it wasn't the pack horse.

He rode back and forth up the mountain, still looking, until he saw horsemen galloping that way from camp. A posse. They'd hang him as a matter of course if they caught him, so he struck out for the top of the ridge and the Benton road.

Chapter Eleven

'We Got To Git It, Gal.'

Dallas Hill emptied her pistol and was reloading when Ox Farrell ran up and grabbed her arm.

'Dallas, you'll hit some innocent fire fighter.'

She tore away from him. 'What kind of a marshal are you? Why don't you do something to stop them?'

Ox was big and slow-thinking. He blinked his eyes a few times. Apparently it hadn't occurred to him before. 'Sure I'll stop 'em. I'll get a posse together and follow 'em. I'll see to it the vigilantes get fetched, too. We'll get that strongbox back for you, Dallas, or bust tryin'.'

He rushed down the street, finding men who were willing to ride. There were twelve in the first group, with more coming, but Dallas knew that most of them just wanted to watch the excitement. Posses were all the same. It's not easy to find men who are willing to risk themselves for somebody else's money.

Ox was gone until midmorning and rode

back escorting a miner who had the bodies of two men in the bottom of a jolting ore wagon. Ox stamped around importantly for a while, letting on he'd felled them with his own guns, but under questioning he had to admit that the raiders had evidently got to fighting among themselves. One of the dead men was known as a cheap gambler and loafer; the other was a stranger.

Dallas said something about Brass's hirelings, and Ox answered, 'No, they ain't. I'll tell you who led that outfit. It was Comanche John. Kelly saw him with 'em. Kelly knew the old Comanche down in Bannack. John was masked, and he had a blanket over him, but Kelly said he'd know them jackboots and his way of sittin' a horse anywhere.'

There was no use staying in town. They wouldn't get the gold back. She rode uphill to the prospector's shanty and waited until noon for John to come. When he didn't, she went on along the Benton road reaching the Frenchman's during the night. There she rested, swapped the saddle to her own horse, and asked for the one Comanche John had left, only to hear that he'd been there already and taken it.

She was on her way again at dawn. Noon found her approaching Flatwillow Creek. A rider had been waiting in the brush, and when she was about thirty yards distant he came out and pulled his horse sidewise across the trail.

She reined in with her hand instinctively resting on the side-hammer pistol, but there were others. She could see them now coming from among the box-elder trees. They'd seen her from a distance and were waiting.

Most of their faces she knew from American Flag. The vigilance committee. She counted fifteen of them. Their leader was a big, good-looking young man named Jim Dekker.

'Hello, Jim,' she said quietly.

'Why, hello, Miss Dallas.' He took off his hat with a flourish. 'You been to the Flag?'

'Yes.'

'You know about the White Palace then. It was tough. We been trailing those road agents that grabbed the strongbox. Left about sunup.'

She looked around at them. This was the first time she'd ever seen the vigilantes unmasked, but there were no surprises. It was common knowledge who they were.

'Where's Brass?' she asked.

'I ain't seen him in ten days.'

'He was in American Flag last night.'

It was a guess, but the quick exchange of glances told her she was right.

Dekker drew a furrow over the bridge of his nose. 'So he was in town! Well, perhaps he had other business.'

She laughed. 'Yes, I know the business he

had. And so should you. You're honest, Dekker. You're just a fool. Nobody can blame a man for that. They're born that way. Brass has been using you to do his dirty work for the last eight months. He set my place afire, or had it done, so I couldn't use it to finance the boat. Then he got worried that I'd have enough in the faro bank to pay off, so he sent his renegades back and grabbed that.'

Dekker's face had turned a shade darker. She'd jabbed a sore spot. Others had been saying he was Brass's dupe; not to his face, but he knew the talk was around town, and it angered him. 'If you want to know who was really at the bottom of it, I'll tell you! It was a man you've befriended. Fact is, we have reason to think you've been feeding him at your own camp. I mean Comanche John.'

She was contemptuous. 'If you think he's there why don't you go out and take him? Or did you have enough of him that night when you tried to hang Pike Wilbur, in American Flag?'

That was another sore spot among all of them, and a rangy, rawboned man named Staples said, 'By dang, that's just what we're going to do. And so there'll be no tip-offs you're going to ride along and watch him stretch rope.'

She'd been waiting her chance. She spurred her horse, but Staples, a tall man, bent over, made a long-armed stab, and grabbed the bridle. He drew it hard around his saddle horn, keeping the frightened animal from rearing, and said, 'Thar! Now maybe you won't be so flighty.'

'Take her gun,' Dekker said.

'Got it.'

He handed it to Dekker, who put it in his saddlebag. 'I'll give it back to you at camp.'

They rode off, following the river rims. The afternoon was hot and utterly still. Dallas had her bridle again, but with men close on both sides she had no chance to break away. Little was said. The men were tired and tight-lipped, sweaty, with the sweat dried over their faces making a fine scurf of salt.

In about two hours they topped a cutbank rim and saw the boat camp shimmering through heat and mirage beneath them.

A sentry called out, 'Who goes thar?'

Rifles and sawed-off shotguns came from their scabbards.

'We go there!' Dekker barked.

'Well, stay put or I'll cut loose.'

She knew his voice. The little Californy man, Hagen. He made the mistake of show-ing himself. Staples already had his shotgun up. He beaded and pulled the trigger. The gun roared, and its heavy charge of buck caught Hagen and spun him around. His gun clattered away. He fell and caught himself in a sitting position. The buckshot had frayed the left side of his shirt. He clapped one hand there, and blood ran between his fingers.

Dekker turned on Staples and cried, 'Dammit, you shouldn't have done that!'

Staples laughed through the smoke of his gun. 'He talked about shootin', didn't he? Well, there's shootin' enough to satisfy him.'

'I told you before–'

'You told it to Brass, too, remember? And what did he tell you, bucko my boy? So you keep ridin'; there's nothing to hold us off that camp now.'

Dallas had leaped down from her horse. She ran to Hagan, who was just shaking off the bullet shock. None of the vigilantes paid attention to her now.

'Spread out,' Dekker said. 'Lyn, you take the upriver side with Nick and Shorty. Carnes, you take a couple of the boys that way. And watch he doesn't swim the river. The rest of us'll hunt the camp.'

They were off downhill at a gallop, leaving Dallas who had her bowie out cutting Hagen's shirt away. He'd been hit by three of the shot, but apparently his ribs had turned them from the vital region of his heart.

He said, 'I'll be all right as soon as I git my breath. Whar is my gun? I'm going down thar after that–'

'Lie still.'

She probed with the point of the bowie and recovered one of the balls. Another had gone straight through and had been caught by the back of his shirt, and the third seemed to have lodged somewhere beneath his shoulder blade.

'Where's John?' she asked.

Hagen managed to laugh. 'They better come at thirteen o'clock if they want to catch that old wolf. He lost some toes in the trap, he has. Benton vigilantes beat 'em here, anyhow. They rode in about sunup this morning, but John must have got scent of 'em because he waren't around.'

Dekker and his men repeatedly searched the camp and combed a mile of river brush; afterward, ill-tempered and still suspicious, they held 'court'. One by one they brought men from the camp in front of them, even the Chinese, but they learned little. Although Wilcoxson and other Pike's Peakers had no fondness for John, they had even less for the vigilantes, whom they associated with Brass's raid. It was sundown when the questioning was finished. They asked for food and, met by Mrs Coppens's invective, they simply shouldered her aside, went through the storeroom, and helped themselves to what they wanted, retiring with it to a camp slightly downriver in a clump of box elders.

'Ye stranglers!' Mrs Coppens kept shouting at them. She calmed down and said to Dallas, 'They know John's been livin' hyar. Reckon they figure on camping until he gits back. I just wish Wilbur was around. He'd

175

put the run on 'em, he would.'

After supper each night it was usual for the Pike's Peakers to sit around a fire, to chaw and swap stories for an hour before hitting the shucks, but tonight they were silent, apprehensive, and they retired early. Only young Rip Timmons seemed unaffected. After the others were gone he sat on an upended nail keg with his banjo and sang in his nasal voice the sad fate of the boy who took work on a wagon train hauling ore across the Sierras to San Francisco.

'Oh, rusty pork and wormy beef,
And bread without the risin',
They fed us even worse'n that,
My Gawd, but it war pizen.'

Finally Mrs Coppens shouted, 'You quit singing that song. I know when something's aimed at my cooking.' So he changed key and, without altering his mournful tempo, sang:

'Comanche John rode to Barmack town
As bold as bold could be,
He laid his hard-won money down
For rum and raw whis-kee.
He shot up five or six saloons
And chased the sheriff, too,
A rougher, tougher woolly wolf
Nobody ever knew.'

Mrs Coppens looked around at the night-black edge of the clearing and said, 'By dang, if that don't bring a whoop and holler out of the old reprobate, I reckon he sure enough is out o' earshot!'

Crouched in the bushes between there and the river, Comanche John heard every word of the song. Hunkered on his boot heels, he rocked slowly back and forth, humming the melody. It was a new stanza, and not wholly based on truth, but top card for all that.

Finally Rip got up, yawned, and stretched himself, so John called, 'Don't look, Rip. Just walk straight up to the cookhouse and take it slow. Tell Miss Dallas I'm hyar.'

Rip did as he was told, and in a couple of minutes Dallas groped her way around through the brush looking for him.

'Where are you?'

'You're nigh stepping on me, gal.'

Close as he was, it took a few seconds for her to locate him in the darkness.

She said, 'You're taking an awful chance.'

'It's my bread o' life.'

'Where'd you go? I waited for you at the top of the ridge.'

'I'm sorry, gal, but when those gents took off, with the strongbox, I put on a horse blanket and trailed along. Thought I might get my hands on it and break free, but the way things turned out I was lucky not to get blasted inside out.'

'Then you *did* ride off with them.'

'Gal, you say that like folks *knew* I did.'

'A man by the name of Kelly recognized you. Now everyone believes the raid was your business.'

'Now that's ornery. Story like that gets out, it'll make a bad verse for my song. Comanche John setting fire to a gamblin' house so he can steal from a gal. By grab, if I hear anybody singing a verse like that I'll riddle him with my Navies. See how hard it is to reform? Well, I reckon I might as well have the meat if they smear me with the taller.'

'What do you mean?'

Instead of answering directly he said, 'We got to git that machinery, gal. I rode down and had a look-see at Brass's camp while we had visitors this afternoon. His boat's nigh on as far as our'n. I wouldn't be surprised if he was planning to put our machinery in it. Offered Far West something extra for it. That'd account for 'em trying to back down on the agreement.'

'I know.' She bit her lip and fought back the tears. 'I can't go to Pike and tell him. Not the way he is. John, what are we going to do?'

'Why, sit tight. You just keep these men humpin' like we were going to git that machinery next Monday. Brass ain't the only one with influence hereabouts. I got a couple o' famous friends, too. Dang it all, what good are friends if a man can't call on 'em in his hour o' trouble?'

Chapter Twelve

Line Up To Be Robbed

Comanche John rode off with an extra horse on a lead string.

'Danged right I got a couple o' famous friends,' he muttered, hitching the Navies at his hips. 'The Colt Brothers, and something tells me they been quiet too long.'

He made a long ride before morning and slept through the hot hours where the trail turned off toward the Big Belt Mountains and Confederate Gulch. He'd thought of taking it, but reconsidered. Instead he rode toward American Flag, reaching the camp about midnight.

There'd been new gold strikes south of there along the Missouri River terraces, and at a camp named Hog Heaven, just over the ridge, quartz ore worth ten thousand dollars a ton was being stamped out in hand mortars, so the town was booming bigger than ever. Saloons and dance halls were aglare and ablare. John had been long without a celebration, and the sounds made him feel good, putting a new spring in his jackboots as he trod the corduroy walks. The street was a steady press of men – mule skinners, prospectors, gamblers, and lesser flotsam of the frontier – none of them paying him the slightest attention.

He stopped in front of a place called The Polka Palace, keeping time to the music that came from the steadily flapping batwing doors. He could see the orchestra on a gilded platform – men playing violins, a zither, and a huge Negro with rings in his ears beating a square piano that had reached the gold frontier after a journey around the Horn by sailing vessel, and by ox team from San Francisco. There were a dozen or fourteen partners – painted women in bright silk dresses – with miners lined up for their turn to dance with them, a privilege for which they would pay a 'sixteenth of gold', or approximately one dollar, together with the usual drink of wine.

He went on, past a half-finished building, bigger than anything he'd seen in the territory. He read the banner in front of it: *Soon Open – Longest Bar North of San Francisco*. Beyond was the Tennessee Hotel and the office of Brass's stage line.

A small, graying man in kerseymere and old fashioned congress gaiters was hunched over a big book inscribing figures, alternately using a quill pen and a blotter.

He looked at John's face with a flat lack of recognition when asked about Kid Sykes, the line's top shotgun guard.

'Last Chance, waiting for a coach.'

'Tonight's coach?'

'Why, it could be tonight,' he said, still putting down figures. 'Or tomorrow, or the day after that.'

John went back and swapped saddles to his extra horse. If Kid Sykes was in Last Chance, John would ride there and watch him. Sykes was a notorious gunman, and they'd be using him to ride guard only on those coaches northbound toward Benton with a heavy load of gold dust.

The road took him through pine timber, past the smaller bar diggings of Midas and Mule Gulch. Freighters had stopped and built fires on both sides of the river while waiting their turns on the ferry. It worked steadily – a wagon one trip and four span of mules the next. John watched for a while, sitting in the shadow, one knee crooked over the horn of his saddle. Then he rode upstream and crossed at the old ford. By dawn he was heading across the desolate flats toward Last Chance.

The camp was somewhat larger than American Flag, and several stone buildings gave it a look of permanency. Main Street wound along a gulch. The saloons and dance halls on both sides had a tired look by the light of morning. Some dispirited customers, men, and a few women with painted, ghastly faces, stood around. Chinese were at work sweeping floors and carrying the litter away in baskets to pan it for the gold dust that had been scattered by a host of drunken revelers the night before. He left his horses at a livery corral and limped on saddle-stiffened legs around to the stage stables.

A skinny little hostler was out front getting a sixhorse team ready for the Virginia City coach.

'Kid Sykes traveling this one?' he asked.

The hostler didn't look around, and a bushy-haired man with a brace of Navies sagging at his hips ambled from the barn, stretched, yawned, brushed hay from his hair, and said, 'Won't do you no good to talk to Ab, mister. He's deaf and dumb. But if you're looking for Sykes, you'll wait a spell yet. He was here at sunup and went down to the Virginny House to bed.

'Which room?'

'I could tell you that, but 'twouldn't be no favor. Man get to snoopin' around the Kid's room and he'll shoot him right between the eyes.'

'I wouldn't like that,' John said after some consideration. 'Do you reckon he'll ride guard on the next coach?'

'To whar?'

'To American Flag.'

'Why, that all depends on things.' His eyes narrowed down showing his suspicion. 'Why do you want to know that?'

'Had an idee o' riding with him. We're old associates from Californy.'

Comanche John found a room at the Overland Hotel, but the bed was too soft, and he tossed for an hour before giving up and spreading a blanket on the floor. When he awoke and looked from the window it was late afternoon. He went downstairs, ate Mormon eggs at a dollar each, and played faro, choosing a spot against the wall from which he could see both doors and the stage office across the street.

The coach loaded and pulled out for Confederate. Then toward nightfall the Deer Lodge mud wagon limped in on a sprung wheel which it had developed on the rough road around Jericho.

Soon after the Deer Lodge coach arrived, Kid Sykes came from the Virginia House and stopped to look at his watch.

Sykes was tall and lean, a bitter-faced man of thirty with a peculiar, lax manner of carrying himself. Around his waist, strapped high, was a brace of Navies with special cutdown barrels. He put his watch back, looked carefully up and down the street, and walked to the express office.

The crowd was dense inside the Overland,

183

and with twilight coming it was hard to see through the smoky front windows. Comanche John cashed in his chips and went outside. Kid Sykes came from the express office at the same instant. For a while he seemed to be looking across, directly at him, but John slouched against the log front, hidden by the solid stream of men. The Kid apparently didn't notice him. He turned, gave his two guns a hitch, and went on up the street.

Here and there one of the gulch walls would plunge so steeply that no room was left to build on the street level, but there were generally strips of bench ground higher up and these were occupied by buildings, long and narrow, often bent to fit the space available. Stairs led up the cutbanks to such places, and quite often there'd be another set of crazy, zigzag steps to the parallel street high above.

The Kid climbed a set of these stairs and entered a saloon with red and blue lamps burning outside. John watched for a while, and when the Kid didn't come right out, walked across to the stage office and asked for him.

'Look for him at Gracie's,' the agent said, glancing up from a stack of express tracers. 'Or at the corral. He might not be back before the coach leaves.'

'He's riding shotgun to American Flag?'

The agent looked up, longer this time.

'Sorry, but we never give out the names of our guards and drivers until coach time.'

'Why, thankee. Thankee, anyhow.'

He went outside, waited until Kid Sykes came down the steps, and trailed him back along the street to the Virginia House.

John watched him go upstairs, and in a quarter minute followed him. A candle burned in a bracket lamp, dimly lighting the hall. There were two rows of closed doors. He walked slowly, listening. Light showed around one of them. He could hear the shift of a man's weight on the floor boards.

'Kid!' he said.

The sound stopped abruptly, and he knew the Kid had stepped aside, fearing a bullet through the panels when he answered. 'Yes?'

'Agent sent me down. Changed their minds about you gunning the American Flag coach. Reckon ye'll take the Virginny coach instead.'

'Are they crazy?' Sykes flung the door open and came to a stop against the steady barrel of John's right-hand Navy.

John laughed at his popped-out eyes and said, 'Why, hello, thar, Kid. What's wrong, don't ye recognize your friends from down Californy way?'

Sykes backed up. His eyes kept making little darting movements, but there was no way to escape the leveled Navy. John followed, and booted the door shut behind him.

'Sure ye recollect me. I'm the one ye missed that time when you and eight o' the boys rode sleeper on that coach from Illini Gulch to Drybone City.'

'Comanche John!'

'Yep, old Comanche John. Still alive and packing his Navies. Ye didn't believe them stories, did ye – hanging me hyar, and hanging me thar?'

The Kid backed until his legs touched the tumbledup bed. He sat down. It pushed his pistols up so the butts were handy, but he had no immediate intention of reaching for them, and to show that, he was careful to keep his hands far forward, on his knees.

He said, 'You keep your grudges a long time.'

'Now that ain't fair, Kid. I don't carry my grudges worse'n the next man. Why, I could have picked ye off that same coach less'n a week later right atop o' the Tom Road Pass, if I'd wanted. I didn't come hyar to be unfriendly. I came to buy ye a drink, but just so's it won't end in tragedy I'd like ye to unbuckle your Navies and kick 'em under the bed.' He waited while the Kid complied, unbuckling the belts carefully, letting first one gun and then the other thud to the floor.

'Thar,' John said, letting his own gun drop lightly in its holster. 'Now you walk yonder to the door and call for a quart of good old 'Nongahela.'

A Chinese boy brought the liquor, and left quickly on his soft shoes without glancing around or saying a word. John poured a couple of drinks, said, 'Hyar's to Jeff Davis,' and the two men drank. They had another, and John asked how long they had before the coach left for American Flag.

The Kid glanced at his watch and said, 'Half an hour, and if I'm not on it they'll know damn well something's wrong and come looking for me.'

'So they will?' John spat tobacco juice, grunting with satisfaction when he hit a knothole dead center. 'Why then we'll give 'em a snort of old 'Nongahela, won't we?'

'Don't push your luck too far, Comanche! Sometime you'll run the string out.'

'Now it is gratifyin' to hear you worrying about my safety!'

'I don't give a whoopin' damn about your safety. I'm thinking about my own. How many do you think you can shoot out of your way if they come up here?'

'Why, that depends on a number o' things, and none of 'em hyar nor thar, because I ain't planning to shoot my way at all. This is a quiet visit. We got half an hour, and that's time for another drink. You pour one for yourself, and make it big, because it'll be lasting ye for a spell. No, none for me. Just you. Thar. Now you lay belly down on the bed, and I'll show ye a rope-trick I learnt

187

from the Cherokees.'

'What the–'

'Git down like I said.'

The Kid obeyed him, and John, using a gun belt, cinched his forearms together across the small of his back. The belt would have held him a few minutes, but John wasn't through. He took the Kid's bowie, tested the blade, saying, 'Like a razor,' and slid it through the belt buckle until its hilt guard caught.

'Just a word o' warning. I'm turning the blade down with her edge agin' your arm, so don't try to wiggle free, because if ye do ye'll git cut, and the more ye fight it the deeper she'll go as the belt tightens up, and a gunman without his right arm ain't much good to himself or anybody.'

John tied his legs, gagged him with a mouthful of blanket, bolted the door, and blew out the candle. He waited a while by the open window. Night life was booming along in the fine style there at Last Chance, and even without the gag Kid Sykes would have had trouble attracting attention.

John lowered himself from the window and dropped to the ground ten feet below. He was in a narrow alleyway between two buildings. There he listened three or four minutes more to make sure the gag was effective, and when no sound came from above he walked to the sidewalk and down to the stage station.

The coach had just been brought around

and they were stowing express aboard. One of the lead horses kept rearing and a hostler had hold of the bridle, fighting him down. A couple of passengers, both men, got in and sat smoking cigars.

'That all?' somebody asked, and the agent, cursing, sent a boy on the run to the big, ornate, ramshackle building that housed the Palace Hotel. In the meantime the driver clumped from the saloon next door, ready to leave, and when he saw he had neither his shotgun guard nor the main group of his passengers he shouted in a brawling voice, 'Whar in hell are they?'

John roosted on a hitchrack across the street, biding his time while the driver stamped back and forth in his heavy horse-hide boots and cursed all phases of the coach business with an astonishing range of epithets. At last five men came from the Palace, so the driver stopped and climbed to his high seat. There he looked around and bawled, 'Now whar in the dirty, dyin' old hell is the shotgun guard?'

John swung up from the side street. 'Hyar I be.'

'Hyar you be! Well, who in hell *be* ye?'

'I be the shotgun guard sent to replace Kid Sykes.' He thrust out his hand. 'Name of Jones.'

'Dave English,' the driver said, still suspicious. But by that time his important passengers were there, and he bent over to look at them. They were Army officers. One of them, a man of fifty, handsome and aware of it, drew up before entering and glared at the lead horse which was rearing again.

'Driver, are you sure you can manage this team?'

English shot a blast of tobacco juice over the rumps of his wheelers and said, 'I'll manage 'em, gineral. You just climb in and let your handmaidens tuck ye to sleep.'

One seat was still empty, and this was taken by a heavily armed man from inside the station. John knew without asking that he was a sleeper, a gun guard posing as a passenger.

Dave checked to see that the doors were closed, then he shouted, 'Git or git tromped!' The hostler let go, and he stood, swinging his long lash, bringing its snapper to a stop with the sound of a pistol shot. 'Git to runnin', you wolf-bait, chaw-tailed Injun mules afore I cut your hides to ribbons.'

People cleared out of the street, and they hit it downhill along the gulch with Dave still standing, swinging his whip. The coach made a turn on two wheels, careened over chuck holes, rumbled across a bridge, and then, with some of the vinegar drained from the team, Dave eased back and had the coach rocking gently as a perambulator.

Now that he could let go his hold on the

seat, the 'gineral' thrust his head from the window and gave Dave a dressing down which he placidly ignored.

'Who be they?' John asked.

'Army men. Big one's Colonel Bentlings, Department of Missouri. He came up from Fort Leavenworth saying he was going to organize the territory against Confederate skulduggery like that ruckus they had over in Oregon, but all they did in Last Chance was have a whoopin' big time at the Palace Hotel.'

'Yankee varmints!'

'You ain't a Johnny Reb, are you?'

'You're damned right I be.'

Dave cursed some more. 'Injun horses, coach full of drunken Army men, and now – a reb for shotgun guard. I tell you, if it gits any worse I'll tell Brass he can take this coach and shove it down the sluice tails o' hell, I'm going to the hills and look for gold.'

After long rolling across the rocky flats Dave turned in at the Signal Butte station for a change of horses.

The sleeper guard got out to stretch his legs, then instead of going back inside he climbed aloft, shoving his sawed-off double gun ahead of him.

'Mind if I ride the hurricane? Them blow-hard Army men are too much for my stomach.'

John had his first good look at him. He was

a heavy, dark man with a droopy mustache. Around his waist was a brace of Navies, and for good measure he carried a Texas derringer loaded to the muzzle with shot.

He stopped with one knee on the seat. He'd just realized that Kid Sykes wasn't there.

'Who are you?' he asked.

'Name of Jones.'

'Where's the Kid?'

'He war laid up in bed. Had a seizure. Couldn't move, even. So as a favor I came in his place.'

The coach entered hills beyond Signal Butte, at first low and rolling, covered with scrubby sage, then rising to steep summits that were patched by bull-pine timber. The road wound endlessly up one gulch after another, and to pass the time Dave English weaved to the wheels bumpy rhythm and sang:

> ''Twas in the early summertime
> Of the good year 'Sixty-two,
> They rode from Walla Walla town,
> Four lads all brave and true,
> Thar was Three-Gun Bob and Dillon,
> And Steve from Lac Grand Ron,
> And last but not the leastwise
> Came old Comanche John.'

The guard said, 'I wish you'd quit singing that thing. It makes me jumpy.'

John drawled, 'Skeered o' the old Comanche?'

'I ain't skeered o' nobody. If that Comanche John ever tried robbing a coach I was on I'd give 'em something to write the last verse to that doggerel with.' He slapped his sawed-off shotgun. 'I just wisht he would get in range. I'd show 'im he wasn't so much. He might be a ring-tailed ripper, but I dare say he'd fill the same amount of hole as the next one with a charge of number two buck in his innards. By the way, Jones, seems funny I ain't run into you around Last Chance before. When'd you hire out with the company?'

'Why, Brass and me had dealings for a considerable spell. But you stop asking questions and keep your eyes on the shadders, because I had a heap of experience with road agents, and right now I feel it in my bones that this coach is about to git robbed.'

'Not with me aboard her.'

'I reckon it will.'

The guard saw the gun in John's hand and started back making a grab to save himself from falling off. 'Why'd you draw that Navy?'

'As I said before, I got a feeling this coach was going to be robbed. In fact, it's being robbed herewith.' John moved back, crouched on the hurricane, bracing himself with one hand between his feet. 'Now I built up a liking for both of you gents, and it would grieve me extreme and fill my heart with woe to put a bullet through ye, but that's just exactly what I'll be forced to do if ye don't take things mighty careful.'

The guard stared in his face. 'Who are you?'

'I reckon you guessed that already. I be Comanche John.'

Dave English had frozen on the reins. He was pulling the leaders back. There was a slight downgrade. He was bringing the lead team up too fast, and the coach, rolling without a break, pushed the rumps of the wheelers. It was an innocent-looking maneuver, but one that might start the wheelers plunging and put all six horses down the road in a runaway.

'Don't try that, Dave.'

'I ain't trying nothing.'

He grabbed the hand brake, making the coach come to a scraping, lurching stop.

The guard still had his sawed-off in his hands, the stock on the hurricane, barrel vertical.

'Git your hands up on the bar'l,' John said. 'Thar. Now drop her overboard.'

The guard was very tense. He slid the shotgun, butt first, over the edge of the roof. A projecting nail was there, just long enough to hook one of the triggers. He hesitated, but John was watching, so he changed his mind and let the gun fall clattering against rocks that had been scraped up from the roadway.

'I'll bother you boys for your Navies, too. And that shotgun from out the boot.'

Colonel Bentlings had thrust his head from the window. 'Driver! What's wrong? What's the idea of stopping every two miles? By my watch we're half an hour late already.' He froze, and his eyes projected when he saw the muzzle of John's Navy a bare six inches away. 'What – what–'

'This hyar instrument with the hole in the end of it is known hereabouts as a Navy Colt, gen'ral. She's all cocked and primed and ready to talk, so if you hanker for American Flag instead of Kingdom Come you keep right on climbing from this coach and tell your boys to follow ye.'

Bentlings was furious, but he obeyed. The side of the road slanted steeply, and he almost fell. He steadied himself with one hand on the door and cried to someone inside, 'No, you fool, not with his gun pointing at me. Come on out!'

One by one they followed him, carefully, their hands up, aware of the gun covering them. John counted them, and said, 'You git down, too,' to the guard.

Colonel Bentlings tripped and sprawled, got to his feet, and shouted, 'This is an outrage!'

'I ain't raged out at anybody, gen'ral, and as long as you keep polite I don't intend to. Line up, boys! Line up so's you'll be able to tell your children and your children's children how ye was robbed by the most famous road agent between hyar and the border of old Mexico, because I'm Comanche John, I'm an old lone wolf from the Rawhide Mountains, I eat chawin' tobaccer when I'm hungry and I sleep with my boots on. I do for a fact, so don't antagonize me, because the sight of a Union man turns my trigger finger jumpin' jittery and it's been nigh onto days o' the week since I had a man for breakfast.'

They were all in a row with their hands up. It was a pleasant sight, recalling old times, and John was satisfied to sit for a while with his legs dangling, chawing tobacco and looking at them.

'Why, this is fine. It's top riffle. Mayhap you boys been riding through Californy and been robbed before. Tell ye what ye do next. Ye take turns, starting yonder, and step for'ard. Shed your guns first, and then empty your pockets. Guns thar, and valuables thar. Share and share alike, that's my motto.'

It took about five minutes. John lowered himself to the ground. The valuables made a small heap – wallets, jewelry, one buckskin sack with a heavy lump of gold dust in the bottom. He nudged the things around with his boot toe and said, 'Why, this is poor scratch coming from a bonanza country like Montana Territory. I wouldn't bother with it.

'Tain't my custom to take much of passengers, nohow, unless, o' course, I run into
one too heavy-loaded for his own good.'

He looked them over while he talked, and
the peculiar sag of Colonel Bentlings's blouse
pocket attracted his attention. He took a step,
keeping his gun back in case anyone had a
mind to gamble by grabbing for it, and
reached in. It contained a heavy gold watch.

He held it by its chain and watched it
swing back and forth. Jewels in its case
made little streaks of red and white sparkle
by moonlight. He pressed a button that
made its case spring open.

'Why, it's later than ye'd think. Big needle's
north and the little one's east by south. And
thar's a little bitty needle. Damme, look at
that little one go!' He snapped the cover
closed and turned it over. 'Something writ
hyar. Dug right in the gold. What's that say,
gen'ral? It's a bit dark for me to read.'

Bentlings had been frightened, but he'd
recovered himself now. He'd taken a breath
and held it so long his face was purplish. He
let it out suddenly, crying, 'Give me that
watch! Give it back to me, you brigand! I
tell you, I'll bring troops here and swing you
by the neck if it's the last thing I ever do.'

'Lots o' boys had an idee to hang me, and I
dare say more'll git it, too. And as for
bringing troops hyar, I doubt old Robbie Lee
will certify the project. Now you ca'm down

197

and tell me what's writ thar on the watch.'

Colonel Bentlings, conquered his rage enough to say, *'Commune periculum concordiam parit.'*

'What's that, Cree?'

'Latin.'

''Tain't swearing, is it? I'm a man o' religious leanings, gen'ral. What's it mean?'

'It means that men will agree when faced with a common danger.'

'And so they will. Why, that's good. By grab, I'll just take this watch along so's we'll have something to remember each other by. And now, boys, if ye'll turn your backs and keep 'em turned I'll clean up the details and not bother you further.'

He carried their guns over and dumped them inside the coach. Then, without ever quite losing sight of them, he climbed back to the hurricane.

'Git 'em running, Dave, and keep 'em that-a-way, because I'd lay money thar's hide-out guns in that bunch, and I wouldn't want you hit by any stray fragments.'

Dave whipped his team to a run and kept them going for a mile, then under John's directions he swung off on a side track that after much wandering played out among some abandoned prospect holes. There John got the strongbox down and opened it, finding upward of five hundred ounces of gold packed in little tin containers bearing the sticker of the Brass Company agent in Alder Gulch.

'Bank-sealed! By grab, that's getting fancy!'

He dumped it all in a buckskin bag and rode off, leaving Dave and the coach, driving the extra horses. It was still dark when he reached Last Chance. There he got his own horses and rode to Confederate. By the expedient of buying chips and cashing them again in one after another of the gambling-houses he secured Confederate dust for the Alder dust that might be otherwise identified, and with darkness at hand he headed up Cement Gulch toward the pass, and thence across hill country toward French-man's Roadhouse and the river camp.

Chapter Thirteen

Comanche John's Law

They'd launched the boat, and John drew up, tired as he was, to admire it. Carry Beal, the hunter, saw him and rode that way, leading his two pack horses loaded with carcasses of antelope.

'Purty, ain't it?' John said. 'Always liked boats. Reckon I'd o' made a sea cap'n if it hadn't been I took to coaches.'

Carry, a leathery, dried-up little man from Kentucky, said he 'lowed maybe the craft looked all right, but the way things were stacking up they'd have to use pike poles and cordelle to move it.

'No engine?'

'Nary an engine, and Pike Wilbur still flat on his back in Benton. I don't expect a man should complain, but I ain't seen a two-cent piece in pay for donkey's years.'

'Ye will, and that directly,' John said. 'Hard times be almost a thing o' the past in this camp. Waal, I reckon I'll see what time it be.' He drew out the watch and let its jeweled case dazzle Carry's eyes. Then he snapped it open, took a sight on the sun, and drawled, 'Yep, it's nigh onto suppertime.'

'I 'low, that's a beautiful timepiece.'

'Why, it is for a truth. Wind her at the end and she ticks in the middle. Got writing on the back, too. Says, "Come ye in perils and don't part it." That's Latin, and it has meaning to it. Even skunks stick together when they getting shot at, or some such. This is a very valuable watch, especially on account of the sentiment, because it was gave to me as a token of esteem by a Yankee high up in the gov'ment. Now, Carry, when I rode off from hyar I promised to secure certain moneys, and I did, so if you hanker for pay I'd advise ye to drift along down and be first in line. I take it Dallas is around?'

200

'She was when I pulled out yesterday.'

Jim Swing had sighted them and came riding around the bluffs, bareback and long-legged on his horse.

'Vigilantes been back?' John asked.

'Gates saw 'em skulking the bush yesterday, but they didn't come around. Still and all, I'd be careful how I showed myself.'

Mrs Coppens stood in front of the cookhouse, watching them from the depths of her poke bonnet as they rode down. She turned and spoke to someone inside the house.

'Can just hear her,' John chuckled. '"Thar's that black varmint again," she says. "Hungry as usual, too." By dang, I et stew on the trail to Oregon, but I never et nothing to compare with the stew that ornery Coppens woman puts out. Ye know, Jim, I'm gettin' on in years to the point whar a day and night in the saddle make me ache from the center swivel both ways, and I been giving thought to settling down. I've about decided that thar's the woman for me.'

'Maybe you decided so. But she says she'll never tie up to another man-varmint, no matter what. Wants to keep the memory of her first husband green in her breast.'

'Coppens? Some Pike's Peak plow-whopper, I 'low. I'm not going to let any husband come betwixt me and my woman. Especially if he's dead.'

Dallas came outside to meet him. He got

down and limped back and forth it few times before saying, 'I got 'er. Ye don't need to worry about paying off that money-grabber up in Benton. We'll fix him a hundred percent.' Then, pretending not to notice Mrs Coppens in the door, he yawned and said, 'How-hum! Guess I'll see what o'clock it is by my watch,' and he pulled it out by its chain. 'Why, it's nigh onto suppertime.'

'You'll eat when sundown comes and not before. Lemme see that watch. You pistol-shootin' scoundrel, if you got that through highway robbery–'

'Stay away from me, woman. Didn't I tell ye I'd reformed and was practically a man o' the cloth, and I don't mean that green cloth they put atop cyard tables, neither. This watch was given to me by a gent who said I was one o' the most persuasive men in the Nor'west. Dallas, come along. I'd like to talk to you private.'

He got the gold-weighted saddlebag down and carried it inside the cookhouse. When Dallas followed, he said, 'Close the door,' and let it fall with a heavy thud to the floor. 'Thar. Cap'n Brass sent it. Decided to pay back what he took off Pike after all. And a few ounces more in the way of interest for the use of it. I'd guess about four hundred percent.'

'You took it off a coach?'

'I took 'er off a coach.'

'If that was an express shipment they

might identify it by assay and—'

'Don't tell an old wolf about covering up his tracks, because the only place they'll catch an assay on that express shipment is in the faro banks over at Confederate. Now half o' this color will be enough to pay off for the engine, and I'd advise ye to get it to Severence up in Benton before Brass guesses what's going on.'

'I'll leave with it right now.'

'And I'll trail along just to make sure he don't charge ye too much brassage.'

Mrs Coppens relented and fed him while the Fenn boy was saddling a fresh horse. The night was far gone when they got to Benton, but a candle was still burning inside the office end of the Far West river house.

'Reckon Severence is still up?' John asked.

'He might be. Either here or at the Steamboat Club. He spends most of his time there in the poker game.'

They left their horses and walked around toward the door. All was quiet inside. Some freight wagons were backed up to the Baker Company platform, and Negro stevedores, fled from their masters in Missouri at the onset of the war, chanted one of their interminable songs while trundling handcarts through the wide doors. Steadily, as an undertone, were the sounds of the river.

A man walked between the candle and the window.

'Severence?' John asked.

'Yes.'

She tried the door, but it was bolted. Severence, although off in another room, heard the sound and said, 'Who's there?'

'Dallas Hill.'

'Alone?'

She hesitated and said, 'I'll come in alone.' Then to John, 'Wait for me here.'

He stood out of sight in shadow as Severence, a tall man with silvery hair in ringlets, came to the door holding a gun. He saw her and looked beyond, over her shoulder, then he stepped back, bowing, and said, 'Your pardon, miss. You understand how things are in this river camp. And so late.'

'Not too late!'

He grasped her meaning, and while the door was closing John heard him say, 'Oh, the steam machinery. Now, there is a problem–'

John waited, sitting on his heels, chewing a spear of grass that grew long and tender with subirrigation from the river. Up the slight rise of bank he could see the line of false fronts, buildings of log, rough lumber, and adobe. A few of the places had run out of customers and were closed, but music and voices floated clearly down from the big two-story palaces – the Alcazar, the Bannack House, and English May's.

Suddenly he heard Dallas's voice. He

couldn't catch her words, but there was a ringing vehemence in them.

He stepped to the door and stood with one hand on the latch, his ear against the panels. Men's voices. A couple of men. He was ready to shoulder the door down, but Severence had neglected to bolt it. He was in a hall smelling of fresh varnish. A door about twenty steps away stood partly open with candlelight streaming from it.

Severence was saying in his courtly, reasonable manner, 'Technically, perhaps, that is true. But you are a long way from civilization, and things have to be done differently. It's not as though this same piece of business had been transacted in St Louis—'

She cried, 'I have the money and I demand the machinery!'

The second man laughed, and Severence said, 'I'm sorry, Miss Hill, but Great Joshua, can't you see? If I could deliver the machinery I would. But I can't. It's no longer here. We had so much tied up in it, and the continued delay – I had to return it on the last boat going down to St Louis.'

'That's a lie! Brass raised our price. That's why you wouldn't make delivery when I offered you the first half according to our agreement.'

'*Brass?* You mean Captain Brazee?'

John stood in the door, but for the second none of them saw him. Severence had his back turned. He stood very tall, his handsome gray head back, his hands flung out. The other man was sitting on a chair with his arms around the back of it. He was squat and powerful, apparently just a little amused by the scene. Dallas had also been seated, but now she was on her feet, facing them.

'You know who I mean!'

John, slouched with one shoulder against the door casing, drawled, 'Why, sure, you know who she means, Severence.'

They spun as though his easy voice had been a knife, prodding them. Severence carried a small-caliber gun, but all he did was get out of the way. The other man lunged up from the chair, so that it fell with its back to the floor, and made a grab for the twin pistols around his waist, but he checked himself, and looked down the barrel of John's Navy.

'Why, you're late,' John said. 'I had ye nailed to the wall from the start. So sit down.' The man righted his chair and sank down on it, so John let his Navy fall back in the holster and returned his attention to Severence. 'You know Cap'n Brass, the handsome gent that organizes vigilance committees wherever he goes so he can hang his business competitors.'

Severence was so pale his skin looked transparent. He'd never seen Comanche John before, but he knew who he was. He put one hand out, and it trembled violently, but he managed to get control of himself and say in something of his old manner, 'Who, seh, are you, bursting into my office–'

'It ain't polite in this country to ask a man who he is. Important thing is, I'm here. Now this gal has quarter-paid you for a steam engine, and hyar she is with the heavy color to pay in full, which is a step more'n she needs to do by the agreement.'

'You can't hold me to that agreement.' His voice had turned to a high, womanish quaver. 'We're a long way from any co't of law that can pass on the validity of that agreement–'

'Court o' law?' John laughed and spattered a stream of tobacco juice, striking the high flare of a brass spittoon with fine accuracy. 'Why, I agree with ye. This is a long way from St Louis, and further'n that from San Francisco. Courts don't amount to much hyar, but don't think there ain't a law, because there is. It ain't carried in a book, it's carried on the hip, and it's the quickest wrist and the closest eye executes it. It's impartial. It applies to everybody – human, Chinee, and Injun. Thar's no writs nor no replevins, and generally not even a rebuttal. She's got six sections and every one of 'em is final and permanent. That's the law we're operating under tonight. Dallas, you go out and git this man his gold dust so we can pay him off.'

'I tell you I can't deliver the machinery.'

'Why?'

'It's not here. I shipped it back to St Louis.'

'That's a lie, and you're welcome to it. I always give a man just one lie. One and a warning. Now you tell me whar that engine *really* is.'

Severence believed him. He suspected John already knew the truth, and if he didn't tell it he'd die. He spoke in a voice that was little more than a whisper.

'All right. Don't draw your gun. I'll tell you everything. He offered me more for it. Brazee. Brass. Whatever you call him. I didn't want to do it. I swear I didn't, but he could make it tough on us. He owns that coach line and a chunk of toll road over the pass. He–'

'Whar is that engine now, at his camp?'

'Not yet. It was sitting here waiting. He had to build a stretch of road down at the Falls. The freight wagons got it loaded this morning, about sunup, but they broke a wheel, and then they had to hitch extra teams to pull over the rims out of town. They won't get it to the Falls before tomorrow night. Maybe not then. Probably–'

'We didn't pass any outfit betwixt hyar and the Falls.'

He cried, 'Then it couldn't be that you even traveled the road.'

It was true. John and Dallas had struck the freight road only four or five miles from town.

John asked, 'How many with his outfit?'

'The freight outfit? Four skinners.'

'How many o' the Cap'n's renegades?'

'A fellow named Shep and three others.'

'Four and four. That's nigh onto eight. More'n we can handle. Dallas, you better swap horses at the feed stable and ride back for Jim Swing and his Californy men. Bring 'em down the freight-road and we'll meet ye thar – Severence and this gent'man and myself.'

'I?' cried Severence.

'Yep, *you*. I could leave ye hyar in only one condition, and that condition would be dead, because otherwise ye'd trot right straight to the vigilance committee.'

They left and sighted the freight outfit late that afternoon. It was still fourteen miles from the upper Falls.

John led his two companions into a dry wash, saying, 'We still got a bit of a wait.'

He dismounted and climbed the side. There, parting a clump of sage, he watched one of the jerk-line strings of horses fighting to pull the sharp pitch of a coulee. The boilers had been loaded on tandem wagons, and at each turn the hind wagon would jump from the road and drag the entire outfit to the bottom amid dust, stamping hoofs, and the cries of the skinners.

'Ain't Brass got an engine already?' John asked.

Severence nodded.

'What's he need o' two?'

'How would I know? I'm just a merchant.'

'You're just a varmint, and don't give me none of your sharp lip. Why'd he bother dragging that outfit hyar instead of just shipping it back downriver, or maybe sinking it to the bottom?'

Westgard, the heavy-set man, grinned and said, 'Maybe he figures on powering *two* boats.'

'You mean he thinks he can get hold of ours?'

'It might be for sale cheap one of these days.'

Severence said, 'Keep quiet, Westgard!'

The mule skinners hitched teams from the other wagon and gave the coulee another try. This time they made it, and stopped for a rest. A jug commenced going from hand to hand.

It was then the renegades first showed themselves – four of them, as Severence had said.

'Now, thar's some hard-laboring boys,' John said. 'Got rested up in the shade somewhere so they could lend a hand lifting thar heavy jug around.'

It was too far to identify them, but he thought that one was Shep, and a heavy man looked like Dillman. A while later two more horsemen came in sight from the direction of Brass's camp, one of them staying, the other turning immediately and heading back. By that time the outfit was rolling again.

Sight of the jug had made John thirsty, but there was no water closer than the river. He slid down the bank, digging his boot heels to check his descent. 'Dammit, I been spitting biscuit dough all afternoon.'

Severence, who had been suffering from thirst, suddenly burst out, *'You're* thirsty! Well, seh, what do you think I am? I'm not young any more. I have to have a drink, I tell you!'

'Hyar's a chaw of tobacco. It'll help.'

Severence mounted his horse and reined around. 'I'm riding to the river. I don't care what—'

'Your horse might make it, but I doubt you ever would. Severence, git hold on yourself, because if you try a break, so help me, I'll carve Sam Colt's initials right in your middle.'

Severence checked himself. He made a dry swallow. 'Are you fool enough to think you can stop him from getting that machinery? Let's go back. I'll pay you every cent I ever collected on that engine – your money and his money, too. How's that for a proposition?'

'It ain't worth a damn.'

'I can't stand it, I tell you!'

John chuckled and said it was peculiar the hell a man would endure in preference to a nice, cool, quiet grave. He remounted. It was an effort after living for most of the past week in the saddle, but once there he seemed to fit. A man grows that way.

'I think we better git yonder to the stage road and meet Jim Swing,' he said.

He found them waiting in a coulee – Jim Swing, Dallas, and eight more.

John said, 'We'd been along before, only Severence, yonder, hankered to let the sun burn some o' that pokerchip pallor off his skin. Whar's Carry Beal?'

Jim said, 'Scouting.'

'Then let's wait. We got time aplenty.'

Carry was back at twilight, a little sun-cured man riding a gotch-eared cayuse.

'I seen you this afternoon,' he said to John. 'Could have kilt you all. Would have, too, if I'd been a man of decent convictions.'

'How many renegades ye count?'

'Five.'

'Five when I last saw, too, so Brass must figure that's a safe margin.'

John led them down coulee as darkness settled. Tracks were dug deeply where the outfit had crossed.

'How far be they?' John asked.

'Four mile,' said Carry.

'At that last big coulee?'

'The Sidewinder? Not yet.' He took a sight at the moon which was just commencing to silhouette the Highwood range. 'They'll be there come moonrise.'

The others had ridden around, and John said to him, 'Take her slow. This is a ticklish job, and not too good a chance of it coming off at best. If one o' them renegades gits loose and raises the camp, we're licked. We might be able to stop Brass getting the stuff, but he could stop us, too, and he's already got one engine. We'll have to get them five gunmen all together and by surprise. The skinners will go along if we jingle some money around. Sidewinder Coulee is the last thing to hold 'em up. Once we top that we'll swing west and cross the Sun River bridge. In case I'm not around, Dallas, you pay Severence off and get a signed paper. Severence has decided he wants to live up to his agreements.'

John chose Jim Swing and Carry to go with him, following the wagon tracks to Sidewinder Coulee. It was quite dark, but they could see the outfit stopped in the bottom.

'You wait for me hyar,' John said, and rode down.

He went at a cautious jog, wary for Shep and his renegades. It was a gamble. If they recognized him the jig might be up. But as he expected they weren't around. Not that close to heavy labor. They were taking their ease somewhere, swapping stories or hoisting a jug of trade likker. He found the wagon boss on his hands and knees, untying the snubbers off the back wheels.

'Whar's Shep?' he asked, getting one leg

crooked over the saddle horn.

The big man stood up. He wiped dirt and sweat off his face and responded with a stream of curses. 'How'd I know where he is, the dirty, shiftless bustard? Supposed to give me a hand on the steep going! Only help they give was to lighten up our load by drinking the water so now we ain't got a drink left. Be you from camp?'

'I be from a heap o' places.' He passed his plug of tobacco over, saying, 'Hungry?' and the wagon boss, pacified, gnawed off a cheekful. 'Whar ye think he'd most likely be?'

'Norris!' he bawled. 'Whar them shif'less gun guards go?'

'Down coulee to dig for water. Said there was some green moss yonder.'

'They too lazy to dig for water.'

John turned to leave, saying casually, 'By the way, Mr Severence will be along directly.'

'Severence *here?* What the–'

'Says he's got some new directions to give ye. You're going by way of the Sun River stage bridge.'

'Well I'll be–'

And John rode back without waiting to hear just what the wagon boss would be.

'Find anything?' Jim Swing asked him.

'Mule skinner 'lows they're down coulee digging for water. There some green moss sign yonder, Carry?'

'Yes,' he said. 'They be.'

214

Carry, a professional hunter, had criss-crossed the country a hundred times, and had learned the best approach to every lick and water hole. He led them for half a mile and dismounted on a slope toward the coulee.

'Cutbank yonder,' he said. 'Twenty-foot drop, I'd say. Some springy ground below.'

'Any brush?'

'Nothing but sage and a little knee-high buck.'

'Why, that's first rate. We'll pin 'em thar. I'll do a sneak down to the cutbank and get the drop. You boys come up from two ways. Not too close I'll give ye some time.'

He went down, crouching to keep off the sky line. Darkness was heavy beneath the cutbanks. A horse blew and jerked his head with a jingle of bridle links. Then a man spoke. Night silence made the voice sound almost in his ear.

'I drunk better water than this out of a cow track.'

'It's wet, ain't it?'

He didn't recognize the first voice, but the second was Dillman's.

He went the last dozen yards sitting, moving from one hip to the other. He stopped and drew both Navies. Slowly things became visible. Three men were sprawled with their shoulders against a strip of whitish bank with their boots out, and the two others were on

215

hands and knees trying to dip seepage water from a hole with their cupped hands.

He waited to give Jim and Carry plenty of time, then he spoke. 'I'll kill the first man that reaches for his gun.'

There were sudden movements of surprise, but nobody caused trouble.

John drawled, 'Why, that's using judgment, because you're surrounded.'

Jim Swing's voice, 'You damn right ye be.'

John moved forward little by little, and sat with his boots dangling over the rocks. 'What's wrong, Shep? Don't ye recognize your old friends from Piegan City?'

Shep was cursing under his breath. He was on one knee, bent forward, hands touching the ground. 'Sure I know you. You're the Comanche.'

'Yep, the old Comanche. Only I got some help tonight. Git your hands up. All of ye. And turn your backs. Carry! You lift the gunmetal off these boys. No use of 'em toting all that weight around.'

Dillman asked, 'What do you want?'

'That engine yonder. And you're sitting tight till we git it to camp whar it belongs.'

Carry got their guns, and after that it was a weary wait as the moon rose and climbed high and the last sounds of the freight outfit died in the far distance.

Chapter Fourteen

Honor Guest At A Necktie Party

It was a gray dawn when they left, driving the renegades' horses ahead of them. Five pairs of riding-boots were hung over the saddles, making John heehaw and say, 'We'll show Mrs Coppens them boots and tell her we bagged 'em all.'

Jim Swing said, 'Too bad we didn't.'

'Should have took their pants, too. Injuns did that to me one time down on the Powder, and the mosquitoes nigh chawed me to death. Anyhow, they won't travel back too fast with all that cactus growing along the bluffs.'

They crossed the Sun and stopped for a while on the far hills to look at Brass's camp.

The boat had been launched. It was a broader, lowerlying hull than Pike Wilbur had designed. Already its chimney was in place, and there were men at work installing bearings in the paddle-wheel timbers.

'Why, they're getting on,' John said. 'They're getting on too damn fast.'

At their own camp the machinery had arrived without further difficulty, and one of the boilers was already being swung into place at the end of a pine-pole boom.

'The supports fit?' John asked.

'Perfectly,' Dallas said.

Mrs Coppens came to the door, saw the empty boots, and cried, 'Heaven help us all, he kilt 'em. Kilt 'em and counted coup. It's one thing to scalp an Injun, and something else to count coup on a *human being.*'

'Durn right I take coup!' John yipped, trying to prod a few bucks from his tired horse. 'I'm tougher'n a raw magpie. I pepper my taters with gunpowder and drink trade likker before breakfast. Lot o' folks ask whar I come from and whar I'm going. Waal, I'm hell-bound from the State o' Ignorance, and I ain't got long to stay, so hunt your holes ye sod-bustin' pilgrims because if I see a Yankee I'll start a cemetery.'

'I'll start a cemetery of my own,' Mrs Coppens shouted.

John stopped his horse and clapped his black slouch hat over his heart, saying solemnly, 'Forgive me, Mrs Coppens. Waren't my fault; it war the upbringing I had. Born in a log shanty without a floor and taught my numbers off a pack o' playing-cyards. I trod the wicked ways, and I been sinful to shame Gamorrah, but think how it would pour ile in some woman's lamp o' righteousness if she'd take me in hand and reform me.'

'I'll reform ye with a blast of birdshot.'

John retired to the bushes and slept. He had a swim in the river, and returned to be served a plate of stew by an unusually solicitous Mrs Coppens. With evening on its way he carved boondoggles with his bowie knife and watched the work as it went on beneath the light of pitch-pine torches. By midnight both boilers were in place, and the heavy engine was being eased down on its supports. Next day, the addition of chimney and paddle wheel made the boat look complete, but a great deal of inside work needed to be done.

That evening a buckboard jolted down from the stage road with Pike Wilbur, very pale and weak, seated beside the driver.

'Pike, you shouldn't be out of bed!' Dallas cried, running toward him, but he brushed away her help and got down by himself.

'I'm all right. I'll never get my strength back lying in bed.'

He unloaded a keg of Kentucky whiskey, called a meeting, and spoke.

'If this thing succeeds, we'll all cash in on the profits. That's a promise. I heard in Benton that Captain Brass's boat would be ready to leave tonight. Maybe it will. Maybe it will steam around the bend in the next hour. Then he'll be first to establish a boat route, and that will win him a lot of advantages. But it won't stop us. There'll be freight enough for two boats, or ten, with gold-

219

quartz discoveries being turned up on every hillside.'

Pike Wilbur had arrived at a fortunate moment, for no other man there had the experience necessary to line up the engine, to bring things in balance, to install the rudder, steering-cable, paddle wheel and drive.

Everything fit. Scarcely a timber had to be shaved down or moved. After a long series of reverses, luck was running with them. They did in one day what they'd expected to do in three. A night and day passed with no sign of Brass's boat, and at supper Pike said, 'With luck we'll beat him!'

But luck for Wilbur suddenly played out. He'd gone almost without rest since his arrival. It was too much for him. He collapsed and had to be carried to his bunk. He ran a fever and lay all night raving incoherently.

John took over the boat. During the carpentry stage his keelboat experience had served him, but the engine to his eye was a baffling mass of heavy wheels and gadgets. As he stood looking at it, Wilcoxson hobbled up on his improvised willow crutch and said, 'Khabo understands the innards of these things.'

'Send him up!'

Khabo, a short, good-natured Pike's Peaker, had served a year as engine swipe on a Mississippi River packet, and between the two of them the final details were completed.

John walked to the house, hoping he could ask a few questions of Wilbur, but Dallas stopped him at the door.

'I got to ask—'

'He's sleeping. You can't talk to him.'

'When can I?'

'Maybe tomorrow.'

'Damnation, tomorrow's too late.' He strode back where the men were waiting and bellowed, 'All right, ye shif'less Yankees! Git some pitch-pine shavings. Kindle a fire thar in the box. Let's git this teakettle to b'iling. I aim to take a boat ride upriver and have me a sniff of American Flag night life.'

Khabo kept twisting a valve here and one there as smoke rolled from the chimney. At last a soft hiss of steam came from the low-set safety valve and he wiped sweat and grease off himself with a rag.

'That's when I expected her to blow up,' he confided, 'but we're over the hump now.'

'Ye mean she holds at the seams?' John did a polka step in his jackboots. 'Yipee! I take back all I said about Yankees. Khabo you're my hero o' the hour.'

It was dark then, and John had some trouble finding the quart of 'Nongahela he'd cached out in the bushes, but finally he did and presented it to Khabo. 'But don't git likkered, because if ye do I'll let it out of your gullet with a Navy slug. By grab, we're just a step away from licking that high Judas and we don't want to spile it now.'

Khabo had a small snort and hid the remainder in the wood rack. 'It'll last me all the way to American Flag.'

John walked ashore directly into the leveled shotguns of the Benton vigilance committee.

'We been waiting for you!' It was their leader, short, heavy-set Jack Hartley.

'What the devil!'

'You'll meet him soon enough, too.'

Hartley came down the slope of the bank. Firelight shone along the barrel of his gun. He peered at John's face and said, 'So *you're* the one! I *did* see you in Fort Benton, then. You had your cheek about you, riding in there when it was broad daylight.'

John had recovered his old, slouched, don't-give-a-damn manner. 'Why, I got as much cheek as the next man, I reckon, but I thought these whiskers hid 'em. Anyhow, why I shouldn't ride into Benton with the light o' day is more'n I can see.'

'We know you're Comanche John.'

'Me? Why *he's* a road agent. A dirty, low ornery coach robber. I'm just a poor pilgrim in search of rest and haven away from the winds of the cruel world. Name's Jones. Moses Leviticus Jones. Right out o' the Book, though I don't expect that would be much in the eyes of a vigilante.'

A tall man stepped from the shadow, saying, 'Jig's up, John.' It was Captain Brass.

Brass, tall and easy-walking, came down the bank with a soft jingle of spurs, and stopped a few steps off, not wanting to place himself between John and the leveled guns.

John said, 'Waal, damme, if it ain't the rattlesnake-in-chief. So you've taken over the vigilantes up in Benton, too.'

The remark stung Brass, but the handsome lines of his face were schooled like a gambler's to hide any show of feeling.

'I have the same concern any honest man would have in hanging a man like you. The Benton vigilantes were looking for you a long time before I ever joined them.'

Firelight glistened on Brass's teeth as he smiled. He enjoyed the scene. He hated John. He hated anyone who defied him, and John more than any man alive because he'd haunted his trail, reminding others of the life he'd tried to bury. Now that he'd run his enemy to ground he wanted to enjoy the conquest.

'You should have been satisfied when you made the break in American Flag. You should have kept going. There's an old saying the Chippewa have that fits this. "A snare awaits the otter that travels the same trail twice."'

'Why, that's good. It's first-rate. Yep, you outfigured me, Cap'n, and I'm not the one to deny it.'

John slouched forward as he talked, keeping his hands – shoulder-high to indicate he'd make no trouble.

Hartley said, 'Mace, take his guns.'

'Why, now, there's no need of doing that. I'll unbuckle these old Navies myself.'

'Keep your hands away from them!'

'You ain't scared o' me, are ye? You and all your bully boys? What sort o' nerve you Benton stranglers boast of, anyhow? Now these Navies are coming off me for the last time, and being a sentimental man I'd like to be the one to unbuckle 'em. If you want to blast me for that, hop to it. You're going to hang me, anyhow. I'd as soon die of lead as rope.'

He reached down very carefully and loosened the buckles. The heavy guns swung down from his hips, and he dropped them on the ground. 'Got a bowie, too,' he said, and dropped it, together with his patent English powder and ball dispenser at one side. He looked at the things, lighted by firelight, and said, 'Thar they be! End o' the trail. Tuck off for the last time. My good old Navies that stood by me through hail and windstorm and Injun cookin'. Like no friends I ever had, except the Parson.'

The Parson was at the edge of the crowd, and hearing his name, burst out in his magpie voice, 'Ye stranglers! Ye cohorts of hell! Ye killers that trample honest folk under your hoofs for the benefit of power and privilege!'

'Keep still!' Brass cried, spinning on him.

'No I won't keep still. Roll me in pitch and

burn me like a martyr, and still I won't keep still. I'll shout out agin' the ways o' the wicked wherever I run into 'em.'

Brass went up the bank with five long strides and struck the old man backhand. It drove the Parson staggering. He sat down. His eyes were glazed and baffled. He tried to get up, but one arm was still in a sling and he fell completely. Some of the vigilantes didn't like it. One of them shouted to stop, but Brass had lost control of his temper. He stepped forward to boot the old man alongside the head, but Mrs Coppens dashed between them with her sawed-off shotgun.

'Git back or I'll—'

But a vigilante came up behind her and wrenched the gun from her fingers.

'How many of these wild females you got here?' he asked.

Another man had already taken Dallas's side-hammer pistol.

'Just the two,' somebody said.

Brass had stopped, high-shouldered and tense. He made no further move toward the Parson, who staggered to his feet.

John said, 'That makes twice you've slugged the Parson. You're the brave one, all right.' The Parson started to say something, but John shook his head. 'No. You just ca'm down. Ye got to take the hand that fate deals ye. No good to struggle agin' 'em. My chips of life are all in the pot, and hyar I am without even openers. I see now that the string has run out and it's time for the Great House Man to take his rake-off.'

'Amen,' said the Parson. He breathed deeply and repeated, 'A-a-men!'

'How soon will the hangin' be?'

Qualey asked, 'You getting anxious?'

'I don't hanker to die, but it seems to be out of my hands.'

Hartley said, 'It'll be now.'

One of the vigilantes was already tying a noose. Hartley stepped over to watch him. He'd supervised the hanging of ten men in the last year, but it was still a grim business and it showed in the lines of his face. He looked around the clearing. The big cottonwoods had been taken out for cabins and boat timbers, but one box-elder tree, larger than the rest, presented a high, overhanging limb suitable for the purpose.

'That one,' Hartley said, motioning for a couple of his men. 'Make a teeter drop. Use one of those planks.'

John said, 'I always 'lowed I'd like to git my drop off the back of my horse.'

'You should be glad we'd go to the bother of making a good drop and not strangle you.'

'Why, I am. By dang, I don't want to sound ungrateful. This is a fine, thoughtful thing you boys are doing for me.'

They tossed the noose over and set it swinging. A plank was tilted in the manner of a child's teeter over the keg Rip liked to use when sitting by the campfire singing his songs.

Hartley said, 'Bring him along.'

John pulled back. 'Hyar, now! I need time for prayer.'

'I'll give you exactly two minutes.'

'Two minutes is a mighty short time for a man to save his soul after traveling the rocky pathway I have.'

'You should have thought of that before.'

The Parson cried, 'He did! John's got plenty o' sin to worry about, I 'low, but he's a white lamb compared with you stranglers. I'd hate to stand in your tracks in front of the judgment seat.'

'Don't argue with the gentleman,' John said. 'Two minutes he said, and we got to make the best of it.'

'Ye want to pray?'

He took off his slouch hat and bowed his head, 'Reverend, I do.'

'Best all-around prayer I know is the one I taught ye when ye hit the sawdust trail at my mission four year ago in Fort Walla Walla.'

John gave it thought and shook his head. 'Dang it, Parson, I learnt that prayer so I could say it backwards and forwards, but I had so much trouble and heartbreak in the world I forgot it.'

Hartley had tested the noose and the drop. He came back and said, 'All ready!'

'It ain't been two minutes.' John drew out the watch and held it, swinging it on its chain. By firelight its case was bright with diamonds and rubies, giving it a spectacular glitter. 'Now hold on whilst I take a sight on the needles of my watch and see just how much time I have.'

He snapped open the case and, with every eye on the watch, hefted the patent powder horn with his boot toe and tossed it into the fire.

It exploded with a sheet of flame and smashing concussion. The air was filled with showering coals.

John simply let the force of it knock him to the ground. The air above him roared with buckshot. He got his gun belts and rolled over. For an instant, with the fire scattered, it seemed quite dark. There were willows beneath him. He lunged, and fell to the soft mud of the river.

He got to his feet and ran. He collided with someone. It was Hartley. They recognized each other at the same instant. Hartley tried to bring his sawed-off around, but John hammered him to the ground with a swing of his holstered Navies.

Hartley was down, flat on his face. John stepped over him. Brush tore at his clothes, but it was concealment, too. The pasture was a hundred yards upriver. He rammed the pole fence in the dark, climbed over it.

Someone spoke his name. He spun around and drew one of the Navies. It was only Rip – the kid.

'Here's your horse.'

He was holding the gunpowder, saddled and ready. There were a Jaeger rifle in a double-loop Blackfoot holster, and Rip's own horse pistol on the saddle.

John swung aboard and said, 'Why, this is fine. But how the tarnation did ye every guess I'd be needing a horse?'

'Knew from your song that Comanche John always gets loose somehow.'

'I been lucky hyar and thar. I sure as judgment have!'

Chapter Fifteen

Full Steam Ahead – To Disaster

The explosion of Comanche John's powder horn brought Pike Wilbur awake inside the house. He managed to sit up and get his feet on the floor. Things blanked out, but when he came around again he was still sitting there. He could hear men shouting and the crash of pursuit through the brush. He got up and made it through the front door, where Dallas found him.

'I'm all right,' he said. 'What happened to him?'

'John? I don't know where he is. They've made a circle around camp and they're closing in. We'll have to do something.'

He started to laugh. He sounded hysterical. 'Help John? I'd hate to be the man trying to drag that old catamount out of the bushes.'

Rip was near the whim-saw platform and heard him. 'Don't worry about 'em catching John. Not combing *that* piece of brush, they won't.'

Brass was furious at the turn of events, and kept screaming orders to the Benton vigilantes until Hartley, angered at having his command usurped, put a stop to it.

Hartley said, 'Anyhow, it's no use. He's gone.'

'And whose fault was it? Who gave him two minutes *to pray?* We should hang that sky pilot. He's as much responsible as–'

'The sky pilot had nothing to do with it. John just outfoxed us, that's all.'

Brass was stiff, his fists doubled, pressed against his hips. He spoke through his teeth.

'Well, what do you propose to do?'

'Keep after him.'

'And leave the boat?'

'Of course.'

'They're all criminals, and you know it. Every man here. They harbored him–'

'Half the people in the territory have

harbored Comanche John.'

'The engine in that boat was taken by force. By highway robbery.'

'They have a receipt for payment in full signed by Severence.'

'Given over for money taken from me by highway robbery.'

'That can't be proved.'

Brass spoke slowly, pronouncing each word just behind his teeth– 'There are some Army men in American Flag. Colonel Bentlings and his subordinates. They were sent out by the Department of Missouri to determine whether this country needs military rule. If you defy me in this; if you let this boat leave shore, I promise to have a contingent of troops in Fort Benton before the snow flies.'

Hartley decided he meant it. 'I don't want to fight with you. Law and order is licked when one vigilante outfit starts fighting with another. I'll keep the boat here until we can settle the whole thing in a meeting with Wilbur, Severence and yourself up in Benton.'

The delay was sufficient, and Brass saw victory after all. He smiled and shook Hartley's hand. 'Sorry, Jack. I've been a little wrought-up over this thing.'

Steam pressure slowly went down in the boilers as the vigilantes kept watch. In the morning Pike Wilbur tried to go aboard and was blocked by the gun muzzle of a big, truculent, red-whiskered man.

'Those valves have to be watched while the steam's going down. If you do anything to destroy this boat–'

Hartley came over and said, 'We're not here to destroy anything. If you need a man on board you can have him there. But just one.'

Pike inspected the boat and went ashore, sending Khabo to keep watch. 'Don't let all the pressure go down,' he said.

There was no work to do and an uneasy quiet settled over the camp. Sensing it, Hartley's men stayed close and watchful. In the afternoon five men from the roving band of American Flag vigilantes rode down to reinforce them. They'd been sent by Captain Brass. One of the newcomers was Staples, and another was a gunman named Herblette who had killed nine men while hiding behind a marshal's star at White River, Oregon. Both of them had been admitted to the ranks of the American Flag vigilantes at the insistence of Captain Brass, and the three others were of the same predatory type.

Hartley knew trouble might be brewing, so he accepted them willingly, even though he knew that in a showdown they would follow Staples rather than himself.

'I don't want trouble,' he told them. 'Stay close to the boat. I don't even want you riding through camp.'

'We'll take care of ourselves,' Staples said from one side of his bitter mouth.

That evening the Parson saddled and rode downriver. He circled back and followed the sky line of a ridge slowly until a man called to him. It was Comanche John.

'So ye did see my smoke signal,' John said, climbing the steep side of a dry wash.

'I didn't missionary amongst the Arapahoes for nothing. Here, I brung you some o' Mrs Coppens's stew.'

John ate and asked, 'Them vigilante varmints still on watch?'

'Yep, they be. Pike 'lows he'll ride to Benton and maybe get the town committee to meet, but it'll take him two or three days and—'

'And it won't do him a pennyworth o' good, anyhow. You git back thar, Parson, and see to it they keep steam hissing through the gauges. I'll lick up the rest of these dumplings and give a thought to what can be done.'

'Don't let it be anything foolish.'

'Seems to me, Parson, I been sensible and careful long enough.'

He took his time with the stew and as darkness settled rode back to the river. From a hill promontory he could see Brass's camp blazing bright from pitch torches. Men were climbing over the boat, and black smoke rolled from its chimney. As he watched, the smoke commenced coming in puffs, showing that the blower was at work. They were putting on a good head of steam, getting ready to leave.

He crossed the river. It was falling with midsummer, but still deep enough so his pony had to swim for about thirty yards in the middle. There'd be plenty of channel for boats.

He circled and came back to the river half a mile below Pike's camp. No torches there. Everything looked quiet. A fire on the bank had burned down to coals, and there was a dull glow from the boat's furnace doors.

A backwater had dried up, leaving logs of many lengths and sizes to dry in the hot drought. He chose a couple, bound them together with a length of babiche from his saddle, and dragged them to the river's edge. Weather had bleached them almost white. He smeared them with black muck, then he stripped, rolled his clothes in a bundle around his jackboots, and put it aboard with his guns on top. Everything was ready. He turned his horse loose with the reins looped to the saddle horn, and pushed the raft out.

He waded a long way through shallow water and finally swam with one hand on the raft, the other used as a paddle and rudder.

He worked steadily to reach mid-river, then he remained still and drifted, dipping his hand only to use it as a rudder.

He cleared a willow-grown point and saw the boat with its shining white stern and pilothouse rising above the long, lapping surface of the water.

He could hear men talking. A voice he didn't recognize said, 'She might look like a white girl, but she ain't. She's Spik.' Another man made some remark, and there was some lazy laughter. Those were the vigilantes, but he couldn't tell whether they were aboard the boat or on shore.

The raft drifted close. He dipped his arm and swung slowly, careful to make no ripple in the water. The paddle wheel loomed above him. He could have got hold of it and climbed aboard, but the risk was too great. His best gamble was down the side, by the deckhouse. He guided the raft away and cleared the stern. It floated very slowly with the flare of the side above. The end of one log touched. It joggled inch by inch along the planks.

Finally it came to rest amidships. That was as good as anywhere. He stayed down for a couple of minutes, listening. Voices came to him. Not close. They were around the deckhouse and on shore. He drew himself aboard the raft and let water run off his body. He could see the deck then. No one moved. He was in luck. That side of the boat was deserted.

He climbed aboard, thrusting his clothes and guns ahead of him, and dressed. It was hard to get the jackboots on his damp feet, but he didn't feel like Comanche John without them.

He walked carefully and drew up close to the corner with his back against the wall. One of the men was only arm's reach away. He was seated with his boots thrust far out whittling on a willow with a barlow knife. He said something, and John knew his voice – Staples, that vigilante from American Flag. There were four others on board with him.

John already knew the positions of the hawsers holding the boat. The first he reached easily and cut with his bowie. Half freed, the boat swung on a slow arc from the shore.

'What was that?' one of the vigilantes said.

'We're moving!' It was Staples. They were on their feet. 'Hey, she's loose!'

'Not yet, but she will be!' John barked.

They spun and faced his two Navies, drawn and leveled. He'd dropped his bowie. He kicked it across the planks. 'Take it, Staples. Cut it loose!'

Herblette, the Oregon killer, had moved to one side. There he thought himself hidden by shadow. He drew the gun from his right hip. Flame leaped from Comanche John's left-hand Navy, and the slug smashed Herblette backward. He was on his feet for two steps, then he hit the rail and did a spread eagle overboard.

John had fired apparently without looking.

236

He was still watching the four men in front of him.

'Cut it!'

Staples sprang on the second hawser – the anchor hawser – and severed it with one chop of the knife.

Men were coming from shore, thigh-deep in the river. One of them sprang and got a handhold along the rail.

A bullet from John's Navy shattered it a few inches away, and he let go.

Guns cut the darkness, their bullets wild thudding the deckhouse and the boat's side as the offshore current swept them faster and faster downstream.

From below, he could hear Khabo shouting, 'What the tarnation–'

'It's all right, Yankee. I'll take care o' things hyar. You git the power on this boat. We're headed for American Flag.'

'I ain't got the steam.'

'Then make it, and make it fast. I got some crewmen hyar for you.' He looked at them, all vigilantes from American Flag, all Brass's men. 'Unbuckle your guns and go below.'

They obeyed and fell to stoking the fire, working the hand bellows.

'When'll we have that steam?' he shouted down to Khabo.

'Maybe ten minutes.'

He walked back and forth, listening to the regular creak and hiss of the bellows. A light twinkled, appearing and reappearing through the trees overgrowing a downstream point. He could hear the rapid *chuff-chuff* of an engine, the splash of a paddle wheel. It was Brass's boat headed for American Flag.

Brass hailed them. 'Staples! You aboard there, Staples?'

'He's here!' John bellowed back. The boat was swinging toward them, so he sent a couple of bullets whanging at her pilothouse. 'He's hyar, but he's too busy for company.'

His bullets made the pilot swing away again. There were half a dozen answering shots. Then the boat cleared a point and disappeared from view. In another five minutes John glimpsed the lights of Brass's camp downriver.

He went below and pointed his Navy at the steam gauge. 'What's she read?'

'It reads nigh on a full head of steam.'

'Then give her a try.'

Khabo got the machinery to turning. There was a lurch when the paddle wheel took hold. John hurried topside to the wheel. He pulled it far over. There was a sand bar to larboard. It grated softly under one side. The boat hung briefly and came free. They were moving upriver.

'Give her more steam!' John shouted.

'That's all we got.'

'Damnation, plug up that safety valve. Git some more pitch pine in the firebox. And stop resting on the blower.' He fired a Navy slug that narrowly missed Staples and gave him a furious burst of energy. 'Thar! That's the way to work a blower.'

Khabo moved the valve weight out to its last notch, and as pressure built up the boat speeded with it.

For miles the channel was deep and regular with John holding a course down the middle. They sighted the home camp and left it behind. The moon, climbing, made the river almost bright as day. At every turn he watched for Brass's boat.

'More steam!'

'She's already blowing from the safety cock.'

'Move the weight out.'

'She's at the last notch.'

'Then hang the anvil on 'er.'

'I don't want to git blowed to Hades.'

'Then hang 'er on and jump overboard. I been hellbound for twenty year.'

Islands broke the river, and somehow he picked a course among them. There were broad shallows beyond. An experienced pilot would have entered such a stretch at quarter speed, taking soundings from the bow, but Comanche John hit it at full steam without incident.

He saw a ruddy light ahead – the glowing furnace doors of Brass's boat. A skiff had been sent ahead to sound out the channel.

'Git your mud scow out o' the way or I'll shiver your timbers and keelhaul ye,' John whooped. 'Damme, this is more fun than I had since the Blackfeet tried to massacre me on the Three Forks.'

It was a race now with Brass piling on steam and holding his lead mile after mile up the broad bends of the river.

An island split the stream. The main channel was a placid sweep to the west, and Brass steered into it, but John swung the other way, breasting a swift current that had cut a course beneath overhanging cottonwoods.

'Pull down your hat, Khabo!'

It was dark there, shaded from the moon. The banks squeezed down; trees threatened to uproot the chimney. They cleared a bar and burst again into the main stream.

The short cut had sliced through distance, and Brass's boat was scarcely a hundred yards off.

'Give her more steam!'

Khabo, streaked with soot and sweat, killed off the bottle of old 'Nongahela and said, 'All right, if ye want more I'll give it to ye.'

'Whar's your help go?'

'Jumped overboard at the narrows.'

'What's wrong with them vigilantes? Whole country going soft? Ain't they got kidney for a little boat race?'

He edged toward mid-river, slowly closing the distance. A volley of gunfire met them.

It drove John to the cover of the pilothouse. He was down, steering with one hand.

Brass had swung sharply toward the far bank. There were shallows ahead, broken by sand bars that almost touched the surface.

'Cut the power!' John cried, and pulled hard over.

It was too late to keep off the nearest bar. He saw that and called for full speed again. The boat, traveling without cargo, rode high in the water, and that saved her. She hit the bar, seemed poised for a second, almost stopped. Then she slid forward with her paddle wheel beating a brownish froth.

The boats swung together again, both at full speed, striving for the narrowing channel, but this time the advantage was with Comanche John, for he was steering across quiet water while Brass had to breast the current.

The channel pinched more and more. It set hard against the bank with only room for one boat. Gunfire from Brass's boat became intense. John could see men crouched at both sides of the deckhouse. He steadied the wheel with his knee and came up, firing with both hands. Khabo was topside with one of the vigilante shotguns and added a double blast of buck to the onslaught.

Unexpected, it sent them scrambling for cover.

'Clear out o' the way!' John whooped. 'I'm half horse and half alligator. Give way! Give way, damn ye. You ain't fighting no gals and wounded men tonight. This is Comanche John, the one they writ the psalm about.'

He was answered by a volley of bullets that tore holes through the pilothouse and showered him with splinters.

The boat was edging past, and seeing that, Brass turned to ram it. Their sides came in contact. Current and interrupted momentum made them swing in an arc. It was rocky bottom just beyond the channel. They struck it together.

John went full length, the Navy gone from his hand. He recovered it and sat up. The deck tilted and he knew the boat was aground. Khabo came from the hatch with a sawed-off gun in each hand.

'Hell to pay now—'

'They aground too, ain't they?'

'Yes.'

'Then it could be worse.'

'They's water coming in. I'm afeared if it hits the bilers—'

Khabo had accidentally showed himself, and a blast of shot spun him a quarter way around. He dived face forward, cursing. He wasn't hit badly. Fortunately he'd been in the edge of the pattern. He was bleeding along the ribs and in one thigh.

John started to rip his clothes off and get at the wounds, but Khabo pushed him away. 'I ain't hurt. Give me my shotguns.'

They could hear Brass shouting orders. The attack was met with a hail of shot and Navy slugs. Men were down, others in retreat. Several of them, however, kept coming. One was a long, scarecrow figure with a Navy in each hand. Shep.

John said, 'Ye been hunting for this a long time, ye squaw-killing renegade.'

Shep saw him, and they both fired, but John's guns were an instant ahead. Shep bent in the middle; his shots hammered into the boards. He reeled, hit the deckhouse, and went down. He was dead with two bullets through his ribs.

John weaved away and kept firing. He no longer tried to hide himself. His Navies filled the night with flame and streaking lead.

'Come on and git me, boys. Come and git the old Comanche if ye have a hanker for entertainment. Nothin' to it. Just like draggin' a badger out of a bar'l.'

Guns empty, he hit cover again. Khabo was there. 'You still around?'

'I'm hyar,' Khabo said, breathing the words out hard while ramming a fresh load into a shotgun. He wasn't measuring anything – merely dumping each barrel part full of powder and filling most of the remainder with shot and wad. 'That'll fix 'em.'

'I'd ruther stand in front of that than behind it.'

'She's a terror both ways.'

243

'Look sharp, Khabo; the varmints are coming on us from the underside.'

Brass had ordered his men into the river, they'd waded around through hip-deep water, and now they were grabbing for the gunwales.

Over the crash of gunfire there was another sound. The high, intense cry of escaping steam.

Khabo shouted, 'The bilers!' and the explosion hit them.

Chapter Sixteen

Double-Gun Parting

The deck seemed to be jerked from under John's feet. Air was sucked from his lungs by a hot blast rushing around him, and the next thing he was fighting up from the bottom of the river.

He popped to the surface, got his breath, and his jackboots dragged him under again. He made a blind grab and found a piece of floating plank. He hung to it, and got his directions.

Current was carrying him. All he could see was water and the night sky. The sky was unexpectedly cut in half. It took him a second to realize that he'd drifted against the side of a boat. He found a fingerhold and pulled himself up. It was Brass's boat. All dark, apparently deserted. A great hole had been torn in its deck and stern, so evidently the explosion had taken its boilers, too.

He rested on the deck; felt for his guns. They were gone. They'd be useless anyway, powder wet. The boat was drifting very deep; its keel kept grabbing at the bottom and slipping free. Upriver along shore, guns were popping, but none of them were aimed his way.

He started around the deckhouse and suddenly a man was in front of him. Captain Brass.

It was as much a shock to one as the other. Brass took a backward step. He'd also been in the river, his clothes water-soaked, clinging so they displayed the powerful muscles of his body. Like John, his guns were gone. Dropped so their combined weight would not pull him down. His hands reached by instinct to where their butts had been, and John said, 'I reckon if we'd had guns you'd have been dead already, Cap'n. But we ain't, and now it's just you and me, fightin' it out with the weapons we was born with.'

Brass checked his retreat and stood, tall and high-shouldered, with hands resting on his hips. He was smiling a trifle – a hard twist of his mouth. The more he thought about meeting John like this, the more he seemed to relish it. 'Yes, just with the weapons nature gave us!'

John seemed slouched and off guard as always. He shuffled forward in his heavy, water-filled boots. Suddenly Brass bent as though crouching to meet him, then his right hand darted back, behind his neck, and a bowie gleamed in the moonlight. He'd been carrying it in a scabbard sewed at the back of his shirt.

John might have retreated and escaped the blade. Instead he dived forward with one shoulder aimed at Brass's abdomen.

The bowie swung down, but John caught the blow with an upraised forearm. His hand closed on Brass's wrist. He was lighter than Brass by twenty-five or thirty pounds, but he was close-coupled and powerful. He forced the knife higher and higher. He sensed the moment when Brass was farthest off balance, then he jerked the man's wrist toward him and down, at the same second going flat to the deck.

John landed on his side. His legs swung in a sudden arc. His water-soaked jackboots struck Brass just below the knees. They knocked him off his feet. John kept rolling and tried to come up with a leg-breaker, but Brass, too, was a veteran of the frontier. He'd lived through other fights to the death. He evidently sensed what was coming. He let his legs go from under him, landed on all fours, and spun free.

He rose and collided with the deckhouse. The unexpected jolt knocked the bowie free. It made a spinning flash in the moonlight, clattered, disappeared in shadow.

Brass looked around for it, but he had only an instant. John was coming to his feet. Brass seemed to be going for the knife. Instead he grabbed a stick of firewood that the explosion had hurled down the deck.

It was a club three feet long and thick through as a man's arm. He brought it around in a vicious arc, but John, diving, got beneath it, so his head took only a glancing blow.

It was enough to stun him. He reeled with blackness rising like a black whirlpool. Instinct made him pitch forward and clinch.

Brass tried to get the club free. It was pinned between them. He let it fall. They reeled along the deck, John clinging desperately, trying to fight his way up through unconsciousness, hardly aware of the blows that Brass was ripping in from close range.

Then, with a full pivot, Brass shook himself free.

John tripped and went to one knee. The boat, drifting, made a slow outward swing, and moonlight brightened the shadows that hung against the deckhouse. The knife was there, its blade shining.

They both saw it, but Brass was in the better position. He pounced on it and stood just as John charged. They reeled backward and hit the rail. Their combined weights took it outward. It hung for a second, then it splintered, and next instant they were struggling deep in the black depths of the river.

Brass still had the knife, and John clutched his wrist. Current was carrying them. John lost all sense of direction. He felt the drag of the muddy water beneath him. Then Brass's wrist slipped away from him.

He rolled, felt the grab of the blade against his buckskin shirt. It had missed. Under water a man's movements were slower. Brass threshed, trying to recover himself, turn himself over for an upward stroke of the knife.

He didn't get the chance. John spread his jackboots wide and let his weight carry Brass face down into the mud.

John's breath was gone, and his lungs seemed ready to burst, but he lay still while Brass was threshing, using his energy. Brass would have to breathe first; breathe the mud and water in which his face was pressed. After a timeless interval, he could feel Brass's struggles become weaker – weaker–

John's ears were ringing. Suddenly he realized that Brass was no longer beneath him. For a second he thought he'd escaped. Then he knew that the current was carrying him.

His boots were too heavy to swim. He

managed to get them against the bottom, and his legs, uncoiling, popped him to the surface.

He blew water and sucked air in his tortured lungs. He was a good swimmer. He knew better than fight his boots and heavy clothing, trying to stay up. He went down again, touched bottom, popped to the surface again. The third time he found footing on a sand bar, climbed, waded waist-deep to shore.

He turned and watched for Brass. Aside for little twists of current the river was placid under the bright moonlight. No one floating or swimming. Brass was at the bottom, half buried in muck. It was the end of him.

John found a log. He sat down and breathed until dizziness left his brain.

He whispered to himself, 'By grab, I ain't as young as I once was. I ain't for a fact. That rangy-tang almost had me whipsawed.'

Far upriver he could still hear the intermittent popping of gunfire.

'Wonder what sort o' ruckus that is?' He was talking to hear his own voice and steady himself. 'No boats to fight over now. Just two heaps o' planks with their innards blowed out.'

He got a chaw off his water-slick plug of tobacco. Then, keeping to the brush, he went up the shore.

Half an hour passed, and the shooting

died. He was getting close, now. He recognized the landmarks, and he could hear the occasional sound of a man's voice. Someone rode crashing through the willows ahead of him and said something. The voice was Jim Swing's.

John said, 'Hey, yonder!'

Jim Swing said, 'Why, damned if it ain't the Comanche, alive in spite of everything.'

'I die harder'n an old tomcat.' He kept moving cautiously forward. 'What's goin' on down hyar?'

'Why, we rode along to get in on the party. Whar's Brass?'

'Eight feet deep and his boots filled up with Missouri River mud. He wasn't a match for the old Comanche when it got down to fightin' horse-and-alligator style.'

Pike's boat was still there. It had been ripped by the explosion, but shoal water had kept it from drifting away.

'Damme, I thought that scow would be blowed sky high, but from the looks maybe she can be fixed up good as new.'

'That's what Khabo says, too. Says the bilers got ripped along the seams, but the engine's as good as ever.'

'They always got repair bilers up in Benton. By grab, we'll make that trip yet. Whar's the Pike's Peakers? Let's get her towed ashore.'

The Parson heard his voice and said, 'That you, John?'

'It's me.'

'Where's the Cap'n?'

'You mean the late Cap'n Brass. Why, he's at the bottom with the catfish.'

'Ye mean he's kilt? Yipee!' Then the Parson checked himself and drew a long face. 'May he rest in peace, or leastwise as much peace as he deserves. "Love thine enemies," the Good Book says, and it's lads like Brass that puts a preacher on his mettle. He's drowned in the river, ye say? Don't suppose thar's any chance of recovering the body? I got a ding-dang sermon to preach over him. Like to say it the same day I marry Pike and Dallas. That'd make the biggest and most satisfying day I had since I first started to minister the Gospel.'

He'd attracted Mrs Coppens's attention, too. 'Whar is he?' She was working her way through brush with her shotgun ahead of her. 'I heered his voice. John, is that you alive after all?'

'Alive I be, Mrs Coppens. Did you hear what the Reverend just said about tying a wedding knot betwixt Pike and Dallas? What d'ye say we make it a double?'

'I already had one shiftless man, heaven rest his poor, departed ashes, and he whar aplenty. Anyhow, if I was in your boots right this minute I wouldn't be giving thought to a wedding. I'd worry about a funeral.'

'Whose funeral? If you mean Brass—'

'I mean your own. The wind blew down from the bluffs just now, and I got a strong whiff of vigilante. That strangling, Fort Benton variety of vigilante.'

'I ain't running from any vigilante.' He looked warily at the bluffs just growing up in the light of dawn. 'But come to consider it, I *have* been a mite long in this country. Longer'n I'm used to. I say a man stays younger if he keeps moving around. Lengthens his life. Somebody got a horse handy? And maybe a brace of Navies? I'd be happy to make repayment as soon as fate drops some honest nuggets in my poke.'

Somebody got him a horse, a sorrel bronc that was shifty and small but ready to travel. John swung to the saddle. Jim Swing unbuckled his own Navies. He said, 'Thankee,' and buckled them around his waist.

Mrs Coppens said, 'Here's something to remember me by,' and handed him her shotgun.

The gift touched John strongly. He made a movement to wipe moisture from the corners of his eyes. 'Why, that's right nice. Mrs Coppens, I'll never hear this old double gun roar but what I think of ye.' As a final gesture he yawned elaborately and said, 'Waal, guess I'll see what time it is by my watch.'

He pulled the watch out by its chain. A bullet had struck it and turned it almost inside out. He held it to his ear. There was no tick left in its tangled wheels and springs.

'Why, the woman's right. It sure enough is time to go.'

He nudged the bronc and set off through the bushes. They soon hid him from view, but his tuneless voice floated back to them as he sang:

'Co-man-che John rode to Yallerjack
   In the year of 'Sixty-two,
   Oh! listen to my stor-ee,
   I'll tell ye what he do—'

The publishers hope that this book has given you enjoyable reading. Large Print Books are especially designed to be as easy to see and hold as possible. If you wish a complete list of our books please ask at your local library or write directly to:

The Golden West Large Print Books
Magna House, Long Preston,
Skipton, North Yorkshire.
BD23 4ND

To Myron J. (Doc) Dourte

MONTANA, HERE I BE!

The brawling gold mining camp of American Flag, Montana is organized and controlled by a showboat trick-shot artist named Captain Brass. Brass and his gang of renegades kept the gold and whatever else was worth anything to themselves and killed anyone who got in their way. Then Comanche John, the legendary gunfighter, rode into camp and proceeded to take Brass's comfortable little empire apart...